I0552244

Zombie Diaries

Senior Graduation

The Mavis Saga

By
R.W.K. Clark

Copyright © 2017 R.W.K. Clark
All rights reserved, www.rwkclark.com
r@rwkclark.com

This is a work of fiction. All names, characters, locales, and incidents are
the product of the author's imagination and any resemblance to actual
people, places or events is coincidental or fictionalized.
Published in the United States by Clarkltd.
Po Box 45313 Rio Rancho, NM 87174
info@clarkltd.com

Edition 1

United States Copyright Office
#1-6140530899
Library of Congress Control Number: 2017907165
International Standard Book Numbers
ISBN-10: 1948312050
ISBN-13: 978-1948312059
ASIN: B07HYCM9CF

/200801

ZOMBIE DIARIES SERIES

Zombie Diaries - Homecoming Junior Year - ZD1
ISBN-10: 0997876778 ISBN-13: 978-0997876772

Zombie Diaries - Winter Formal Junior Year - ZD2
ISBN-10: 0997876786 ISBN-13: 978-0997876789

Zombie Diaries - Prom Junior Year - ZD3
ISBN-10: 0997876794 ISBN-13: 978-0997876796

Zombie Diaries - Summer Break Junior Year - ZD4
ISBN-10: 1948312034 ISBN-13: 978-1948312035

Zombie Diaries - Fall Semester Senior Year - ZD5
ISBN-10: 1948312042 ISBN-13: 978-1948312042

Zombie Diaries - Senior Graduation - ZD6
ISBN-10: 1948312050 ISBN-13: 978-1948312059

CONTENTS

ACKNOWLEDGMENTS

I dedicate this novel to my wonderful readers and for all the amazing people I've met and those I haven't. To my family and loved ones, all your support will not be forgotten.

This book was made possible by reviews from readers like you.

Thank you

R.W.K. Clark

CHAPTER 1

Shanice Hall adjusted her body on the lounger and moaned with pleasure. The warm sun overhead was beating down on her lovingly, warming her ice-cold flesh, taking away the chill that never seemed to disappear. Even when her skin was warm, the cold still settled in her veins and in her bones; she just couldn't escape it, and never would.

She loved the yacht, and she loved the ocean. It made life easier for her in so many ways. For one, she was sure that the police were searching tirelessly for her in the States; Mavis wouldn't have let her get away without running straight to them. Because of this, Shanice simply postponed her plans for revenge. By purchasing the yacht and floating casually off the coast of Jamaica, Shanice realized that the sheer vastness of the sea did a wonderful job of keeping her hidden. She would stay there indefinitely, with Brad in tow, and let things cool off for a long time before returning to have her way with the little Mavis. This time she would have her way. In the meantime, Shanice would enjoy a long vacation at her dead parents' expense, and she would also enjoy the flesh of the foolish who were so easily lured onto her gorgeous yacht. Disposal was easy; just dump them into the waters and the sharks took care of the rest.

"Would you like another cocktail, my gorgeous lover?"

Shanice turned to Brad, who stood about ten feet away holding a frothy pink creation with an umbrella sticking out of it. She smiled and nodded in agreement as she thought of meeting him on the beach the fall prior. He was a beautiful specimen of a man at twenty-five, and he would continue to look good forever, thanks to the little bite she delivered to his buttocks on the night of their first date. As she took the cold drink from him, she remembered how she told him what she was, what he would become, her true identity, and how they would be together forever. Literally! At first, Brad had been angry and scared, but as he went through the initial sickness, his fear began to pass, and once he fed for the first time, all apprehension was gone for good. Just like Gunnar Reed had been, Brad was the perfect companion, at her beck and call, and she would take care of him forever.

"I thought I would take the Jet Ski to shore and bring back a couple of juicy guests for our nightly party." Brad leaned his shoulder against the doorway he stood in and sipped his drink. "You could stay here and relax; let me treat you for a change."

Shanice sipped her drink and placed it gently on the table next to her lounge chair. "You know, normally I would argue with you, but you have become so adept at knowing my taste I think I'll let you do just that. What time do you plan to leave?"

"In two hours," Brad replied. "For now, I think I'll just hang out here with you and bask in your glory."

Shanice loved it. "You are a sweet talker, aren't you?"

"I try to be."

Brad sat on the lounger next to her, lowered his sunglasses from the top of his head to his eyes, and lay back to soak up some warmth. He didn't speak; Shanice taught him early on that she liked to spend a lot of time in thought and introspection. The reality was she was constantly planning Mavis' demise; the process in her mind never stopped. It was an addiction, an obsession, and she didn't feel complete unless she was doing just that.

She was going to get her, alright, but it wouldn't be for a while. When she had first killed her parents in Tuscany and assumed her mother's identity in the States, she had done little to no planning in regard to her revenge. That had been her worst mistake, and she knew it. Had she planned and executed that plan properly, Mavis would currently be a guinea pig in a laboratory somewhere, miserable and alone. Death was too good for the stuck-up little hussy; eternity under a microscope would serve her better.

But she found one thing to be very vexing indeed: at the current time, Mavis was going on with her life. Sure, her best friend was likely heartbroken over the death of her boyfriend Shawn, and that likely weighed on Mavis as well, but it wasn't enough. She was attending school, hanging with her own boyfriend Matt, and enjoying her life.

The sickening part, at least to the normal human onlooker with moral standards, was that Shanice was living high on the hog, and she was doing it at the total expense of those who had once loved her very much. She saw herself only as the victim, a poor high school girl who was misunderstood from the very beginning, who had been horribly mistreated by one Mavis Harvey. A girl who not only got her in trouble and eliminated her best friend, Candy Wilkes but the girl also stole her very life by making her a zombie.

Regardless she had to admit that she loved being one of the undead. It had turned her already cold heart into one that was frigid, and that enabled her to make her plans with no apprehension whatsoever. Undead or not, that was something she could live with, and she could do it with happiness and a sick sense of contentment indeed.

"Here's to us, Brad," she said out of the blue, holding her drink out to his so they could make a toast. "Here is to the completion of our plans and the happy living-out of our eternity together."

The pair clinked glasses and drank, then Brad said, "I love you, Shanice."

She smiled, but it was more of an amused smirk. "I'm sure you do…"

CHAPTER 2

"Okay, class. Excellent job today! I am especially impressed with the improvements all of you have made since last class, and I want to see the improvements keep coming!"

Master Sheng was the instructor of Mavis and Matt's Kenpo Karate class, which they had started taking only a month after Shawn's death and the last attack of Shanice Hall. Kim was now attending too, but she had only begun last month. It took Kim quite some time to get over her grief long enough to even get out of bed, which was around November. After that, her parents put her into therapy to deal with the loss of her first love, and now she seemed to be doing much better. But, she was bent on revenge, and that revenge had motivated her to join the class with Matt and Mavis. Surprisingly, she was coming along wonderfully in the class, making great leaps and strides at a very rapid pace. Mavis knew she was driven by hatred, but sometimes hatred was all one had to keep them going.

Kim had also taken up a new "hobby" of sorts: she had begun hinting around to Mavis that she wanted to become a zombie. At first, it was just insinuations she gave, but slowly and surely Kim became more and more persistent, though Mavis continued to refuse. The last thing she wanted was her friend, who had been so full of happiness and life prior to Shawn's death, to be brought down by being one of the undead. Mavis told her that she was going to have to deal with Shanice, and the grief, in the usual, normal human way. Kim would pout, let it go, and then move on, but only for a while. She began taking Kenpo in an effort to defend herself, and kick Shanice's bony rear if ever the girl showed her face again.

So, together, they attended classes three evenings a week, and they were all doing very well. They had all made a secret pact to get their black belts and stop Shanice once and for all, even though none of them knew where she was, or even if she was still alive. Something inside of Mavis told her that Shanice was alive and well, and her friends trusted this feeling. Together they pressed on, training and practicing at every free moment so when the time would finally come, and it would, they would all be ready.

As they stood in a small group, wiping sweat with towels and drinking water, Kim decided to bring up the zombie thing again.

"You know, if you changed me, none of this would be needed," she said to Mavis in a low voice. "I think it's ridiculous that you won't help me in this way. I'm your best friend, and I feel like you're letting me down."

Mavis stopped sipping her water and gave Kim a stern look. "I've told you time, and again, this isn't something anyone should hope for. I won't play a part in murdering you, which is exactly what I would be doing."

Matt added, "Kim, you're going through a very hard time. You are going to have to accept that this is the best way and that Mavis loves you, and she has your best interest at heart. Besides, if she won't change me, why would she change you? Think about what you're saying."

Grabbing her towel and water, with a pouty look on her face, she turned to Mavis and said, "I'll meet you in the car." Storming off, she didn't look back.

"I don't know of anything that is going to ease her pain but time," Mavis told Matt. "She still isn't thinking clearly. She is so bent on getting back at Shanice that she is blinded by hatred."

"And heartbreak," he added. "Be patient with her, Mav. We're really all she has." She knew he was right, and she gave him a grim smile and a nod of agreement.

After a moment, they walked out into the bright, sunlit day and took a breath of fresh air. Mavis could see Kim sitting in the backseat of the convertible; she still had that pouty look on her face, and from where Mavis was standing, she could see that Kim's eyes were rimmed in red. The girl had been crying once again; it was something she spent a lot of time doing lately. But could she be blamed? She and Shawn were planning to be married right after high school graduation, and now all of those dreams and plans had gone up in a puff of smoke, thanks to Shanice and her now-eliminated sidekick, Gunnar. Mavis expected the tears to continue for some time, at the very least they would last until far after graduation, and Mavis planned to be there for her friend through it all.

As she and Matt climbed into the convertible, Mavis turned to Kim. "Are you hungry? Do you want to stop at Chinese Chang's for a bit of food?"

Kim sniffled and wiped at her eyes as she thought about the offer. "Um, yeah, I suppose. I'm not one to turn down a good meal, even though Kenpo has helped me to lose fifteen pounds. Yeah, let's do it."

"Good," Mavis replied as Matt pulled the car away from the curb. "My treat, okay?"

Kim didn't answer, and Mavis took that as acceptance. The three of them made their way to Chang's in silence; Kim was in deep thought, while Mavis and Matt let her think in peace. It was important that they let her grieve at her own pace, that much Mavis knew, and neither of them would interrupt her process. But it didn't take long to reach the restaurant, and before long they were seated comfortably.

All of them opted for the all-you-can-eat buffet, so as soon as the waitress gave them the okay, they headed to fill their plates with tempting Chinese delights. Hopefully, the food would lighten the mood and the conversation. Then they would be able to get on with their Saturday without sadness.

It was May, and graduation was in only three-and-a-half short weeks. Mavis and Matt were both excited, but Kim held back any happiness she may have felt. To her, the end of the year represented something that would never be, now that Shawn was dead. Mavis knew that someday that would change, but for now, they would all have to deal with it.

"What are your plans for tonight, Kim?" Matt asked lightly as they all sat down with their food.

Kim spread her napkin over her lap and shrugged. "Homework. I'm putting extra effort into Trig; Shawn nagged me constantly about that class, and he would have wanted it that way. How about you two?"

Mavis replied, "I'm working on a year-end psych thesis, and Matt has a bunch of stuff to catch up on as well. Plus, he has to work at the packing house tonight, so from here it looks like we'll all go our separate ways. Just promise me you'll call me if you need to talk, Kim, okay?"

"Sure thing," she replied, but Mavis wasn't convinced that she would.

They ate the rest of their meal with small talk used to divert Kim's attention from the one missing thing that was always on her mind. When it was finally time to hit the dessert line, only Mavis and Matt went up for a plate; Kim stayed behind, which was not only unusual, it was unheard of. But she waited patiently for her friends to finish their sweets without complaining, trying her best to maintain a pleasant effect and contribute, no matter how minutely, to the conversation.

Twenty minutes later, Matt pulled the convertible up to the Coleman house. Both he and Mavis turned to Kim with half-smiles on their faces.

"Don't forget to call either of us if you need us for anything, Kim," Matt told her. "Anything at all."

Kim shook her head. "For the tenth time, I will call, but I'll be fine, okay? Stop being a worry-wart over me and we'll all be fine in the end, okay guys? I know you're worried, but I'm not going to do anything desperate. I have a plan, and dead people who kill themselves can't carry out plans."

Without another word from any of them, Kim hopped out of the car with her duffle bag and made her way into her house; she didn't look back. Mavis looked over at Matt and shook her head. He understood and gave her a pat on the leg. Both of them were worried to death about Kim Coleman, but all they could do was let the girl get through her pain and make sure that she knew she had friends if she needed them.

Soon, Matt was pulling the convertible into Mavis' driveway. His old car was parked at the curb, waiting for him to head home and then to work. He handed over the keys after fetching his own duffle out of the trunk.

"You think she'll be okay, right?" he asked Mavis.

Mavis nodded. "She'll be fine. We just have to learn the balance between giving her space and supporting her when she needs it; it's a fine line to walk."

Matt leaned in, and the two kissed slowly and softly. "I'll stop by tonight after work and drop your little snacks outside your bedroom window. Are you going to Grandma Cabot's tomorrow?"

"Yeah," Mavis replied. "It's spring planting time, remember."

"Well, I'll pop over there to help after I wake up from work. They're having me work graveyard tonight since it's the weekend."

They gave each other another kiss, then went their separate ways. Mavis used her key to get into the house, even though both of her parents' cars were there. Ever since the Shanice thing last fall, her parents had made locking the house a habit, even when people were home.

"Mom... Dad... I'm home!"

She yelled loud enough for them to hear her from anywhere in the house, then made her way to her room. She planned to shower and then hit the books before supper that evening. The next two weeks at school were going to be filled with finals, which she really wasn't worried about. She had passed her SATs with flying colors, making her entry into Ohio University in Toledo a shoo-in. Matt, too, would be attending Ohio U. He would be studying Medicine, which he solidly decided on after the conflict with Shanice, and it didn't hurt that his girlfriend was a zombie as well. He wanted to study science so he could possibly determine what had happened, what went wrong, and try to find an antidote of some kind. Mavis was sticking to her original plan: she would study Child Psychology and work with children from troubled families, though she had no idea where she would practice as of yet.

"We're in the back," Jane Harvey yelled back. "Supper at 6:30!"

Mavis smiled. "I'll be there!"

So, she dropped her things off in her room and went to the shower, hoping to wash away the bad, sticky feeling of Kim's sadness so she could get on with her night, but it seemed that no matter how hard she scrubbed, the feeling just wouldn't go away.

Mavis cried tearlessly for her lifelong friend as she stood beneath the falling water.

CHAPTER 3

Sunday was Grandma Cabot's day, as it had been for most of Mavis' life. An exception were few; caused by Shanice's chaos or emergencies, special events, or funerals. Today was to be a day spent tilling, mowing, planting, and weeding. It was very important to Grandma Cabot, Jane's mother, to have her garden looking better than any other on the block. After a day of hard work, she would reward her family with the best meal known to mankind, whatever it may consist of.

Matt joined the family right around one in the afternoon, and he took over the mowing so Todd could run the tiller. With the four of them working while Grandma Cabot sat on the patio coaching them and crocheting, the day flew by fairly quickly. Before they knew it, they were all sitting at the dinner table filling their plates. As expected, Grandma was the one to bring up the Shanice situation first.

"So," she began as she plopped a huge pile of mashed potatoes on her plate, "has anyone gotten word from police about that little monster that has managed to hurt so many people? Such a shame, the things she has done. I don't think I've ever been so disgusted in my entire life, and I just wish someone would put a bullet right in that girl's head. Something is seriously wrong with that child."

Matt and Mavis exchanged glances. Something was wrong with her alright, but neither of them was about to clear the air on what that was specifically.

"No, Mom," Jane replied. "She seems to have fallen all the way off the grid. But the good news is that the murders have stopped. I'm starting to feel a little safer every day."

"Mm-mm-mm," Grandma said with a disgusted shake of her head. "I don't care if the murders have stopped. The point is, they're going on somewhere else if she's alive. She must have been born with murder in her blood, and that is so odd, considering that her father was one of the best doctors in Greenville at one time."

Todd washed down a bite of fried chicken with a drink of milk. "Well, you never can tell about people, Mom. I mean, some come from horrible families and succeed greatly in life, while others come from outstanding backgrounds and end up like… well… Shanice."

"Well, give me five minutes alone with that girl," Grandma said, using her fork for emphasis. "I would turn her over my knee and give her a thrashing she wouldn't forget!"

Now Mavis and Matt smiled at each other and kept their heads down so no one would see. Just picturing Grandma Cabot paddling Shanice's rear-end was just too much to picture. Both of them had confidence she could get the job done.

"What seems to be so funny, kids?" Grandma Cabot never missed a beat.

Mavis jumped, startled at having been caught with a smile on her face during a serious topic. "Nothing, Grandma. I was just… just flirting a little, that's all."

Grandma Cabot's eyes went from Mavis to Matt, who sat there nodding like a bobblehead. "Fine, but perhaps you should both pay better attention to what is going on and being said so you don't appear to have a heart as cold as that of the girl we are discussing, hmmm?"

With serious looks, both kids turned their full attention to their plates.

The adults continued with their conversation, mentioning their concerns over the fact that Shanice had not yet been captured, and they were still waiting for her to rear her ugly head when it was least expected. Instead of joking, Mavis and Matt paid close attention to the rest of the conversation. The adults were right; there was nothing to laugh about, nothing whatsoever. It was best that they, too, keep their ears and eyes peeled for the safety of everyone.

It wasn't until twilight that the Harvey family and Matt Morgan left Grandma Cabot's, making sure she was locked inside of her home securely. Mavis was exhausted, and tomorrow was a school day filled with testing and review. She wanted to go home and just fall right to sleep, but she had to have something fresh and bloody in her belly. The night before, Matt had brought her a double portion, since he would not be working Sunday night. She thought she might eat a bit of pig brain before turning in.

By eleven, Mavis was laying her head down on her pillow, and by five after the hour she was dead asleep, even snoring loudly. She dreamed of the battle with Shanice at Donnelly Park at the start of the school year, but in her dream, Shanice didn't get away with Shawn. Mavis and Matt had saved him, and he was alive, happy, and at the top of his football game that season. In her dream, Kim was happy, and she couldn't stop talking about her June wedding.

When the alarm went off early Monday morning, Mavis woke, happy for only a split second before realizing that it had all been nothing more than a dream. Her heart sank as she rose to eat some raw meat, shower, and prepare for her day. None of it was real; Shawn was dead, and Kim would be as sad and miserable today as she was every day. Thanks to that monster Shanice Hall, there would be no June wedding for Kim Coleman.

CHAPTER 4

Shanice broke the ocean water cleanly, took a deep breath of fresh air, and ran her hands through her hair to rid it of some of the dripping water. Grabbing the ladder which led up to the yacht, she began to climb, and soon planted her feet firmly on the deck and grabbed her towel. As she dried her hair a bit better, Brad came around the corner and stood watching her with a smile on his face.

"Always looking so good," he muttered, smiling. "It's amazing to me how you can maintain with so many obstacles against you with this zombie thing and all."

Shanice gave him a smile. "It's all about the makeup and the sun... just saying. After all, look at you; I've managed to keep you looking mighty tasty yourself. The girls just flock around you."

"Makes it easier to go do our grocery shopping, wouldn't you say?"

Shanice chuckled. "Yeah, but considering the fact that we need couples, having men with them most of the time seems to be a bit of a hindrance, but you still pull it off just fine."

She padded over to her favorite lounger and

plopped down, draping her towel from the back of the seat before doing so. As she put on her sunglasses and turned her face to the sky, she said, "Now go on, cutie, and bring me one of those pink drinks with the cute little umbrella."

Brad didn't answer but left immediately to do her bidding. She warmed beneath the sun, even dozing off slightly as she daydreamed about the evening's meal. She was in the mood for Mexican; they always had a bit of spice about them that no other ethnicity seemed to have. She particularly enjoyed that, and lately, it seemed that their meals had been strictly of the Caucasian variety.

"How about Mexican for dinner tonight, Darling?" she asked as Brad appeared and placed her drink on the round stand next to her. "What do you think?"

"Hmph," he replied, sitting down himself. "You know I'm not one for spicy food, but maybe I can find something for myself that has a bit more of a mild aftertaste to it."

"Feel free," Shanice replied. "Whatever you feel will satisfy your appetite. After all, you're the one doing the grocery shopping."

Typically, on a nightly basis, Brad would go to shore and hang out at one of the cocktail lounges on the beach, eyeballing the couples that hung there as well. Eventually, he would choose an ideal pair, one man and one woman, and he would befriend them. Before long, the conversation would turn to the yacht he and his "girlfriend" owned, and he would casually drop the fact that they were planning to party all night long, and would the pair care to accompany him back out to sea? They almost always said yes, and soon, supper would be on its way. Shanice had gone in only one time, and she actually had worked much faster and more efficiently than Brad, but Shanice was lazy by nature, and she'd rather send him. After all, he never failed, he just took a little longer.

The two sat together in content silence, a heavy metal song playing lightly through the speakers. When Brad had finished his own drink, he abruptly rose and took a dive into the ocean. Shanice paid him no mind; as a matter of fact, she rarely did. She would rather keep to herself and keep their relationship as platonic and professional as possible, unless it came to sex, of course. Her black heart found it easy to use him and walk away when she was finished, even though it consistently seemed to hurt what little feelings the man had. Brad shouldn't take it so personally; she had been like that with everyone, including her own parents and friends, all her life.

Shanice's thoughts shifted to Mavis when true feelings crossed her mind. What a weak-willed female, especially for a flesh-eater. It made her sick to think about someone having so much power and wasting it on schooling and love and the like. But none of that was her problem; as a matter of fact, the only problem she had was the elimination of Mavis, and that was a long way off into the future. But there had to be a way to find out the girl's every move, to discover what her plans were so that when the time came, there was no delay. Shanice wanted to be ready when fate dropped Mavis into her lap. Being the way she was, Mavis wouldn't be prepared for the blindsided attack at all.

Then it hit her: a private detective! Why she hadn't thought of it before was beyond her. But she thought of it now, and immediately she rose to her feet, casting a glance toward shore to see how far out they were. Satisfied that her cell phone would get a sufficient signal, Shanice began to search on her phone for private detectives in Jamaica, which they were currently off the coast of. She scanned the names of the detectives that were available in the area, scrolling as she went. Shanice didn't want just any detective, she wanted one who was male, good-looking, single, and therefore easily manipulated by her womanly wiles. She would offer to pay all of his expenses in addition to his fee, and then, when the job was over, she would have him for a snack.

After tapping on several detectives and reading their web pages, she settled on a handsome man of around thirty. He had longish brown hair, clear blue eyes, and wore a very tasteful suit and tie that couldn't have been cheap. His name was Sonny Maneli. Hmm, she thought, an Italian. It seemed to her that he would be an easy mark, and he would likely taste gourmet as well.

In only seconds she had him on the phone, smooth-talking him and filling him in on the job she had in mind. She presented it as a case of infidelity on the part of her boyfriend in Ohio, and let the detective know that it was vital that she knows what this girl was doing, in great detail, until further notice. She used the name Miss Hall and told the man that she had unlimited resources, thanks to the deaths of her mother and father. Shanice let him know that she would be taking care of him entirely during the job and hoped that he could dedicate all of his time to her case alone, if at all possible. Before they wrapped up the call, she made an appointment to go inland and meet with Sonny the following day for lunch, her treat. Hanging up, she smiled broadly; she couldn't have been slicker and smarter if she tried.

"Who were you talking to?"

Brad's voice came from behind her, tinged with a bit of jealous insecurity.

"A private detective," she said as she sat back down on her lounger. "It's going to be a while before we are able to take Mavis Harvey out completely, and I need to know her every move between now and then. Make yourself another drink and stop being so possessive; both of us know I belong to no one but myself, Bradley."

He obeyed, bringing her another drink as well. The two of them got on with their day, relaxing and chatting until it was time for Brad to head to shore to fetch their supper. Nothing they talked about really mattered, nothing ever mattered to Shanice but herself, and nothing ever had.

R.W.K. Clark

CHAPTER 5

It was the weekend once again, and Matt pulled up the car in front of the Coleman house and turned off the ignition. He turned to Mavis, a look of concern on his face. The pair had just finished their Kenpo class for the day; it had been a special Sunday class, which was unusual, considering that they never had classes two days in a row. But their instructor, Master Sheng, was going to a two-day conference in Cleveland and had to cancel their Monday evening class. Matt had been happy because that meant he could pick up full-time hours at the packing house that day; usually, on Kenpo days, he only pulled three-and-a-half or four-hour shifts.

But the fact that Kim didn't show, even though she knew about the schedule change, was of great concern to both Matt and Mavis. She was so determined to get into shape and be able to take on Shanice that she had never missed a class before, and she worked diligently, even at home, to perfect her skills. So, out of concern, Mavis had called her directly after class, only to be told by Mrs. Coleman that Kim had isolated herself in her room all day, crying and refusing to eat. Mavis shook her head, disgusted with herself and her thoughtlessness; she should have known.

"It's prom, Mavis," Mrs. Coleman told her. "It just occurred to her that the dance is next weekend, and she just can't bear the thought that Shawn isn't here to attend with her. She is crushed, and I don't know what to do for her. She is refusing to go; heck, she is refusing to even try to get over this at all!"

Mavis suggested that she come over for a few moments to try and help, and of course, Kim's mother readily agreed, so here they were. As they stood in the living room discussing Kim's state, Mrs. Coleman held back tears of concern. Her eyes pled with Mavis for help for her daughter.

"Are you sure this is a good idea, Mav?" Matt asked. He was sitting on the edge of the sofa at the Coleman house, a look of worry on his face. "I mean, maybe pushing her to heal too fast will do more harm than good."

Mavis looked over at Matt, knowing he had a valid point, then she glanced down the hall toward Kim's room. She could hear her friend's muffled sobs. "I know, Matt, but Kim is my friend, and right now I feel like I'm all she has. I'm the only person, besides you, who really knows what happened and truly understands."

Matt nodded. "Okay, Mav; you know best. I'll wait right here for you."

Mavis took a deep breath and started for the hall. She stopped and turned to Matt and Mrs. Coleman once again, telling Matt to be careful because none of them knew where Shanice was at all; it was to their detriment to be too lax. Finally, after another deep breath, she made her way slowly and quietly to Kim's door.

"Mavis, I am so glad you are here," Kim said in a hushed tone as she wiped at her nose with a tissue and rushed the girl through the door and closed it quietly behind her. "My mom called you, didn't she? Or did you just come on your own?"

Seeing the pain on her friend's face made Mavis feel like crying, but she knew no tears would come. All of this was her fault, and she knew it. If she hadn't become a zombie, or bitten Shanice, none of this would be happening. Mavis would have thrown up right there if she wasn't so worried about staining the Coleman carpeting.

Mavis had to say the right thing to maintain Kim's trust. "I was worried, and Matt and I were just talking about coming to check on you. Obviously, it was a good thing I came; you need to talk, Kim. You need to vent, listen to advice, and start taking some action other than just thinking about revenge and practicing Kenpo, you know?"

Kim gave her a mild glare, then the tears came again. No wonder Mrs. Coleman was at the end of her rope. Kim was out of her mind!

"Hey, Kim," she said softly as she took a seat at the foot of the bed. "I'm here to say I'm sorry. And that it's okay for you to be mad at me over all this." Kim had just laid back down on her bed after unlocking the door; her eyes were so red from crying that they were puffy

and almost purple. The room was in complete disarray.
Clothes were strewn everywhere, plates, glasses, and
bowls of half-eaten food were around the bed on the
floor, and the room smelled stale and musty.

Mavis asked, in nearly a whisper, "Can we talk?"

"Of course." Kim's voice was flat and sad, no voice
inflection or enunciation whatsoever.

Mavis moved closer to Kim and cleared several
wrinkled items of apparel out of the way with her hands,
somewhat apprehensively, and with a wrinkled nose. At
last, she came across an empty plastic straw still stuck
through the lid of a convenience store super-drink,
which she tossed in the over-filled garbage by the desk,
and then she sat back down after flashing a second look
at the rumpled bedspread. Once she stiffly sat, still
glancing around her for wet spots, Mavis tried to relax
and focused her eyes on her friend.

For a long time, the two of them just sat in silence;
Kim waiting for Mavis to talk, and Mavis wondering
what to say. It was one of the most uncomfortable
times Mavis could remember between them in nearly
twelve years, but as Kim's friend, it was essential to stick
it out. Finally, Kim broke the silence.

"So, what's up? I suppose you're here because I
missed class." She spoke in a monotone, with no
enthusiasm, but surprisingly enough, Mavis could hear
the sarcasm in her voice. It oozed rich and thick like
molasses or the pancake syrup at Grandma Cabot's on
Sunday morning.

Mavis shrugged and glanced around again at the

mess that Kim was surrounding herself in. "That's part of it, I guess, but only a small part; I mean… skipping class is just skipping class. I'm worried about you; Matt is worried too, and your mother is at her wits' end, Kimberly. What can we do for you to make this better?"

Mavis knew, deep inside, that Kim was depressed, yes, and that terribly. But it was "situational," this depression. It was grief-based and terribly painful, she was sure, but Mavis also knew that Kim was stronger than the monster she was wrestling. Grief had become a part of their lives.

Without moving any muscle other than her tongue, and keeping her eyes on her own bare feet, Kim replied, "You could bring Shawn back, that's what you could do. Prom is coming, and I won't be going. I won't be marrying him, either. And I certainly can give up any hope for a future with him in it." She turned to Mavis, a clear sneer of resentment on her face. "How would you feel if it was Matt? Huh? How would you feel, Miss Perfect Mavis Harvey, Zombie Extraordinaire? Huh?"

Tears welled up in Kim's eyes once again, and she buried her face in her mascara stained pillow and began to sob silently. This display of sarcasm and anger was the most Kim had ever directed at her best friend, and it overwhelmed her immediately. Mavis, too, was taken aback by her friend's words, but she knew they were spoken out of sheer pain, so she did her best to ignore the spite that blared from them. Other than that, Mavis didn't know what to do, so she did the only thing she could: she scooted forward, curled up behind her best friend, and held her while she cried.

Kim cried for some time. It seemed like every time she was about to get it under control, she would begin again in full-force. Mavis said nothing, only held her and comforted her as best she could, though she knew that there was really nothing she could do to make things okay. Only time could do that, and even though several months had passed, it seemed to her that little had improved. It didn't matter; a true friend remained patient through the hardest and most difficult of times. There was no bringing Shawn Maher back… ever. He was gone. Kim Coleman had to let him go, along with all the hopes, dreams and plans they had together. It was the only way for the girl to keep putting one foot in front of the other so she could make it through the life she had to live.

After more than twenty minutes, Kim finally took a deep breath, and her crying subsided. Mavis slowly sat up and took her original place at the foot of the bed, still waiting for Kim to speak first. Just when she thought the girl never would, the words began to come, and they came out in a rush.

"You know," she began, "I want you to realize that I really don't blame you. I mean, not that much, anyway. You didn't want to be a zombie… I know that. And when you bit Shanice, I know it was out of self-defense. I mean, how could you know something like a bite would make her like you? But sometimes, when I'm alone and thinking too much about Shawn and all of this, I do blame you for something. You have the power to make me like you, so I can get back at her and help you take her down once and for all, but you refuse to help me. You won't do what you can to make this better for me, and that makes me so angry I could just scream."

Before responding, Mavis thought briefly about her response. "Kim, there is so much more to be than what I am—living forever if indeed I will. There is a constant daily fight to do the right thing, to be the opposite of what Shanice is, to keep from hurting those around me, especially those I love… like you. There are the cravings, and the skin conditions, and the hiding and sneaking from my parents. There is the guilt I carry around over Jeff Deason and Colin Handley, not to mention the junior prom. There is a constant feeling that I deserve to die or to be a guinea pig in a lab. These are all the things I don't want you to suffer through. This is why we are taking Kenpo; this is why we are doing what we can, doing what is right, to defeat this enemy."

"But she stole Shawn from me, Mavis," Kim whispered. "I think that simple 'defeat' is too good for her."

Mavis understood completely, but only because she had eaten two of her own boyfriends, putting herself through the same grief and more. Because she understood, there was nothing she could say to try and change her friend's opinion or emotions on the topic. Kim was right; simply "winning" over Shanice was just not enough. Simple revenge wouldn't even be the tip of the iceberg of what she deserved, and that would be the same if the revenge weren't simple. Shanice Hall had run around the Toledo and Greenville area making victims over and over, at every turn. Not only was the entire city permanently scarred, but many of them had lives which were so devastated by her actions that they moved away, far away, and a couple of family members left behind had even committed suicide. There was nothing about the situation that so much as suggested that Shanice deserved anything less than death herself. She was a monster, a rabid dog, and she needed to be put down.

It was then, for only a fraction of a second, that Mavis allowed the thought of giving in to Kim's request and giving her the bite. In that tiny shard of time, she actually pictured her and her best friend pursuing the vile Shanice together, with a single mission in mind, both as zombies. But just as quickly, Mavis came to the realization that she could have no way of knowing what kind of zombie Kim Coleman would be. What if she was uncontrollable and lacked conscious altogether? It was simply a risk that Mavis could not take, no matter how tempting. She would not do it, no matter what the circumstances, and no matter how much sense Kim made with her reasoning.

"Kim," Mavis finally replied, "I want to scream too, and I blame myself entirely for Shawn's death, whether you understand that to be the whole truth or not. I can't tell you how sorry I am. But he is gone, as terrible as that is, and we are still here. We can either spend the rest of our lives hiding and crying and feeling sorry over the situation, or we can let it make us stronger, strong enough to take control of the situation, the right way, and make it right for his sake, and for the sake of the entire city."

Kim looked at her thoughtfully. "You're right. I'm not the only one who lost here, am I?"

"Not by a long shot."

After a long sigh, Kim wiped at her eyes with the back of her hand and asked, "So, what's next? I gotta get over this, and the only way to do it is to put one foot in front of the other; I just gotta. What's next, Mav?"

"You get up and start taking care of your business," Mavis replied, matter-of-factly, "starting with cleaning up this room." She wrinkled her nose, and Kim chuckled. "Next, you do the same thing tomorrow; you get up, look your best, hold your head high, and take your butt to school. Then you practice Kenpo with Matt and me. You hit the books, and you go to bed so we can do it all over again. We'll roll with the punches and go with the flow, and soon the day to face Shanice will come."

"But what about when it hurts so bad I can't stand it?" Kim asked, embarrassed.

Mavis put her hand gently over Kim's. "Then you find a place to be alone, or you grab me, and you let yourself cry. When it's over, you keep going. It's the only way, Kim. Otherwise, you may as well curl up and die."

Kim nodded. "I got it, and you're right. Time to buck up." She paused and looked around her room. "I don't suppose you wanna donate some cleaning time, do you?"

"You'd suppose right," Mavis replied with a shake of her head and a belly laugh. "Matt's waiting outside; I gotta go. But when I come in the morning to take you to school, this room needs to look, and smell, a lot better."

"You got it."

The two girls hugged long and hard, and finally, Mavis found herself climbing into Matt's car, a smile glued to her face.

"I take it things went better than expected?" he asked.

Mavis leaned over and planted a quick kiss on his lips. "We may be at the beginning of getting our Kim back again."

Matt smiled and pulled away from the curb. "Finally."

The two drove off in silence, the feeling of relief tangible in the old, musty car.

CHAPTER 6

Monday came faster than the blink of an eye, and for the kids, it was a perfect day. A new beginning, for all three of them, but particularly for Kim. Both Mavis and Matt were apprehensive about picking her up for classes, as they really didn't know what to expect from her mood-wise. But as it turned out, she was not only looking less pale and tons happier, her room was spotless as well.

"How are you feeling?" It was the first thing Matt asked as he pulled away from her house. "I mean, you look good; maybe you feel just as good."

Kim smiled. "I have to be honest: Mavis said a lot of good things to me yesterday to encourage me. But there was one thing she said that really struck a chord and let me know that I was thinking all wrong."

Mavis turned and looked at her in the backseat. "What was that?"

"It was the thing about feeling sorry for myself and curling up and dying or something like that." Kim had a faraway look in her eyes as she recalled the conversation as best she could. "It just made me realize that Shawn would want me at my best so I could do right by him…

with the two of you. I decided right then and there that no matter how much it hurt, I had to pull myself out of the pit." She looked Mavis in the eye and mouthed the words "thank you." Mavis winked back.

"So," Kim continued her voice a bit lighter. "Classes, then Kenpo practice, then homework, or the other way around for the last two."

"Kenpo before homework," Matt said. "I can study during my break at work, but I can't practice Kenpo, or they'd have me committed… see what I mean?"

The girls laughed, then Mavis suggested, "So, Kim, you and I should do our homework together after Matt hits the road. I can drive you home; what do you say?"

"Perfect!" she agreed. "I've been trying to really improve on Trig, and I've come a long way, but there are a few things I could really still use help with."

"Plans are made then." Mavis reached over and turned up the volume on the radio slightly, and all three of them began to sing the popular song pumping through the speakers. So what if the entire week would be studying and tests?

They were on the verge of new beginnings, and Shanice Hall was nowhere to be seen.

∞

Sonny Maneli watched the girl climb into the shabby car and took as many stills from the video he was shooting as possible. He got plenty of good photos of the actual target, Mavis Harvey, the slender Goth girl who had gone to the door and gotten the other girl for school.

When the car had pulled away and was out of sight, Sonny put down the camera on the seat next to him and slowly pulled away to follow, keeping a good, safe distance behind them. Today was only the first day of his assignment, and so far, so good. When he got off the plane in Toledo the night before he thought of how long it had been since he'd actually been in the States. He hated it here, but he had been raised in the Bronx, and this little suburbia looked as though it had little to nothing to offer a man like him. He was grateful that the kids had been so easy to track, so he didn't die of boredom his first day there.

True to her word, Miss Hall had wired one hundred-thousand-dollar advance right after their meeting. Upon completion of the assignment, which was open-ended at the current time, he would be compensated. In the meantime, all expenses, including socializing, were completely covered. Today, while these kids were in school after he got some shots of them entering the building for the day, he would look for a small place to call home for a while. His day would be full and productive, not to mention sinfully easy.

Sonny got to the school and parked at the curb just in time to get a bunch of shots of the three of them laughing their way into the building. Oh, to be a stupid kid again, with nothing more to worry about than finals, dances, and graduations. If he had known the true heart of the situation, he might have run screaming. But Miss Hall had told him that the girl was an old rival who was messing around with her boyfriend, and the Goth kid was whom he assumed she was referring to. It wasn't like the chick was married to him or anything; after all, he was in high school! But for the money he was making, he just didn't care.

The kids disappeared into the school, and Sonny drove away, whistling an old tune as he went. He would stop, have breakfast and coffee with a local paper. Time to find a place to call home, at least for now.

CHAPTER 7

"I'm telling you two, if I hit any harder, I'm going to break my little fingers!"

Kim was holding her right hand, or mostly cradling it as if it were a whimpering infant. She was the one whimpering, however, and most of it was funnier than it was pity-inducing.

Mavis had her hand over her mouth to keep from laughing, while Matt bellowed his laughter aloud. "Look, Kim, it's just like Master Sheng says: you have to punch through. You have to look past the pain. You know what I'm talking about. You have to see it."

"All I'm seeing is stars and little birdies flying in circles over my head from the pain!" Kim plopped down on the sofa in the Harvey basement, which also served as a rec room, though rarely. "You go, both of you. Take your turns and show me how it's done. I know I'm running behind the rest of the class, but maybe if I see your determination and action I can get my second wind, you know?"

Mavis shot Matt a glance, but he was too busy snickering to pay attention to what was being said. "Fine," Mavis replied. "I'll go first. But you'd better be ready, Mr. Can't Get Enough."

"What?" Matt asked, sputtering through his dying laughter.

Mavis rolled her eyes. "You'll see."

With that, she walked up to the two vices which held the inch-thick board up in the air. They weren't to "karate chop" the board; they were to punch right through it. It was a difficult exercise indeed, but one that Mavis had pretty much mastered. Matt got lucky now and then, but he still needed work, too. Poor Kim, on the other hand, had come up with nothing to date but bloody, skinned knuckles. Mavis always made sure to really glob up on the vapor rub during their classes and practices; the smell of blood sent her out of her mind, so she took proper precautions at all times.

Mavis took her stance and stood before the board, which in her mind was doing no more than taunting her, begging her to split it right in the middle while telling her she could not. She blocked out all sounds, smells, and other distractions, and set her focus hard. Next, Mavis began to concentrate on her breathing, and before another five seconds passed, she drove her fist through the wood with a single punch and a loud cry that accompanied her exhaling breath.

As she stood and observed her handiwork, Matt and Kim sat in silence, staring at the splintered, destroyed board. They both shot glances at Mavis, who was still staring at Matt. She had snapped the thing like a crisp cracker.

Matt whispered, "That was the best break I've ever

seen, Mav."

"Better than anyone," Kim added. "Almost better than Sheng's."

Kim's statement was enough to evoke a massive bout of laughter from both Mavis and Matt. As soon as the girl realized what they were laughing at, she lost it too. Sheng was a Kenpo master, and Mavis merely his student. But even while she was laughing, Kim found herself wondering why. As she let out another round of guffaws to match those of her friends, she looked back at the rack and the broken board; she had been right! It was certainly the cleanest break she had ever seen.

Her laughter abruptly stopped, and she put a hand on a shoulder of each of her friends, who were still rolling, complete with tears.

"Um, you guys, we shouldn't be laughing, even though that was funny," she said. "Look, I wasn't kidding. That's one sweet break, Mavis."

As their laughter turned to giggles, then slowly died to nothingness, both of them looked over at the rack. The very sight of the board and its break was enough to help them both get control of their laughter. Kim was right; it wasn't just as good as Sheng's, it was better.

Mavis stared at the display with her two pals in silence, her mouth slightly agape. "I did do a pretty good job," she whispered. "It's… it's perfect."

Both of her pals nodded their heads in agreement but said nothing.

"You know, it makes sense though," Mavis continued in a normal tone. "Not that I think I'm better than Master Sheng, which would be foolish. It makes sense because I have felt so strong lately; it's like I have so much energy and strength that sometimes it feels like I'm going to burst apart."

Matt turned to look at her. "I can't wait for you to show Master Sheng. Just last week you were busting your knuckles with the rest of us. Now you're pulling off single-punch destruction all of a sudden."

"I don't know why though," she muttered, her voice filled with confused wonder as she shifted her gaze to her right hand, turning it over and inspecting both sides closely. "I mean, I'm eating and exercising the same; I'm not on any vitamins or supplements. But I feel like I could take on the world, and I feel like it a lot lately. I wonder what's happening if whatever it is might be a bad sign instead of a good one."

Matt gave her a chuckle. "I highly doubt it. Look at it this way: if you are even half this good, or feeling half this good when we track down Shanice, she's going to be in a world of hurt."

Mavis nodded absently at him. "I wonder if I've had this strength all along and it's just now showing because that's where my focus is."

"Good theory," Kim replied with a shrug. "Makes about as much sense as any other explanation."

Mavis suddenly snapped out of it, smiled, and turned her attention to Matt. "Your turn, big guy. Remember?"

His smile faded as he recalled the fact that he, too, had to demonstrate the board punch for Kim, as Mavis had. He stood up and took the broken board from the rack, then replaced it with a brand new one. Stepping back, he got into position, squinting his eyes at the long piece of wood as if it were his life's enemy.

"I'm gonna tell both of you girls right now that you'd better not expect anything as good as the demonstration we were just given," he said, his voice steady as he gained his concentration.

Mavis grinned and crossed her legs to get comfortable. "Just hit the thing, Mathew."

After sticking his tongue out at her in response, Matt turned his full attention to the task before him. Soon, he was inhaling and exhaling like a pro, and before the girls knew it, he delivered his first punch. He hit the board squarely in the middle, but it didn't break. A small smear of blood showed on the wood, but it was no big deal.

Mavis and Kim stayed silent, watching Matt as he prepared himself for another strike. The second blow was a failure as well, and Mavis could see red rushing up his neck and onto his face. She felt bad that she had broken the board so quickly; now Matt felt like he had something to prove.

But instead of letting his nerves get the best of him, Matt closed his eyes, got his breathing under control, and repositioned. He went through all the motions, but this time he put all thoughts of "beating" Mavis out of his mind. The third punch he delivered was smooth and clean, and it broke the wood nicely.

Matt stood, both scrutinizing and admiring his work, while the girls sat on the floor with their eyebrows raised. After exchanging glances of approval with Kim, Mavis offered feedback first. It was always nice to set the bar when it came to criticism.

"I think you did a great job; it's a clean break for three hits." Turning his eyes to the broken board the way a judge might look at a criminal, she added teasingly, "Three punches... I did say three, didn't I?"

Matt threw an evil glare over his shoulder. "Three or not, I think it's a job well done, considering what I put the thing through."

Now it was Kim's turn. "Well, since I am the third and final person with an opinion, I'll call the final shots on this one. Matt, it is an acceptable break, but you definitely need to work on narrowing down the number of hits needed to get the job done. I give it a six."

"You're up, Kim," he replied with a smile.

"Hmph," Kim added. "I don't know what you're smiling about; Mavis just beat you like you were the girl."

Now it was Mavis' turn to join in the banter. "You don't know what he's smiling about? Are you sure about that?"

Kim's eyes shifted back and forth between her two friends, her cheerful look fading into one of quick concern. "No... I don't know. Stop teasing now. What is it, Mav?"

"Oh, nothing big." Mavis held her hand out in front of her and pretended to inspect her nail polish. "It's just that it's your turn again..."

CHAPTER 8

Sonny Maneli took the bag of fast-food burgers and fries from the pimply girl at the drive-thru window. After tossing it carelessly on the stained passenger seat of his new jalopy, Sonny handed a wadded-up ten-spot to the kid. With a smirk, he threw the car into drive and screeched off.

"Keep the change!" he screamed over the sound of the tires on the asphalt.

As he turned right onto the main strip, Sonny reached down and turned up the radio as loud as it would go, which wasn't very loud at all. An old song pumped through the only speaker that worked: the one set inside the driver's door. He began to bob his head as he aimed the car toward his new apartment if it could really be called that.

He had scored the place on his first viewing, right after he left Westside High that morning. It was a dumpy little place, fully-furnished, complete with dust and bugs, he was sure. All the utilities came with the rent, so all Sonny had to buy was dishes, soap, towels, groceries, and beer.

At an even three-hundred dollars a month for rent,

Sonny would have lived in a treehouse. Sure, this little lady client of his had been very generous in retaining him, but Sonny had more important things to do with his money than hole up in some fancy, overrated place that bled him dry. Yeah, he had gambling to do, some broads to find, and a lot of drinking to imbibe in. So, since the rent was so cheap, Sonny paid six months in advance and went about his day.

He had waited for the kids to get out of school and managed to get some pretty good photos of all of them and their respective homes. At one point they all went into the home of the target, Mavis Harvey, and they were all dressed like some kind of karate kids. He made a note that they were likely studying martial arts. Other than that, the boy had left and went to work that afternoon at a meat plant, and it wasn't for another two hours that the other girl finally came out of the Harvey home. She had still been wearing her karate clothes, and she was carrying her school books in a bag over her shoulder. Sonny used that time to follow her home and get some extra shots.

∞

Sonny squealed his tires as he whipped his massive car into the complex parking lot. Grabbing his bag of greasy food and another bag with a six-pack of beer in it, he bounced out of the car and be-bopped all the way to his dented front door.

Once he was safely locked inside, he glanced at his food, which now sat on the small, round kitchen table.

Still wasn't quite time to eat; he had to call his client and update her on the day. But he could have a beer, and a beer he would definitely have. Can in hand, he plopped down in a holey, overstuffed chair and dialed Miss Hall's number on his cell phone.

That phone call would prove to be the easiest one of the entire project. It was only day one, and it took him all of five minutes to tell her all about the kids, their photos, his new place, blah, blah, blah. Before he knew it, they were hanging up with promises of speaking again soon.

When the food and half the beer was gone, Sonny pulled the Murphy bed out of its hole in the wall and collapsed on top of it, fully clothed. In seconds he was snoring like a buzz saw, a long stringer of spit running down his left cheek. He cleaned up nice, but in reality, Sonny Maneli was a pig.

R.W.K. Clark

CHAPTER 9

Tuesday was a day Mavis had been looking forward to all year: the class trip for her psychology course was scheduled for that day, and she and her classmates would spend from the second period until the sixth at Greenville Medical Center. The main focus of the trip would be the Psych Department of the hospital, as their treatment ward, and they would be meeting the psychiatrists and psychologists that put the unit together and helped keep it standing.

But they would also be getting a full tour of the hospital, from the ground up, and they would have lunch in the cafeteria there. While Mavis was excited about the actual psych tour, which included some light lecturing on child psychology, she was looking forward to the whole tour even more. She had lived in Greenville her entire life, but had only been inside the hospital a handful of times; it would be interesting to check out the place while learning about the topic that was to be her major course of study in college.

Her mother sent her out the door with Matt that morning with more than enough money for lunch, and whatever else she desired. She was practically on the edge of her seat on the way to school, and during her first-period class. By the time the first-period yearly recap was over, the teacher had looked like she was ready to leave for the day already, and she gave the students the last ten minutes to chat quietly amongst themselves.

The main conversation going on was a predictable one; prom, which was not far away. Most of the girls were talking and giggling about what they had bought to wear to the event, while the guys discussed the chances of another mass murder taking place. She heard comments about how cool it would be, but most of the guys were bent on being the hero of the situation if some killer got to them during the dance. While Mavis hated the fact that the junior prom had been such a disaster at her hand, she found the things the boys were saying to be very amusing. At this point, Mavis was fully confident that she would be able to enjoy her prom without incident by simply sticking to the tactics she and Matt had come up within the last year. There would be no prom night massacre this time around.

It seemed that the bell would never ring, but when it finally did, Mavis was the first one out the door. She made a beeline for her locker, where she deposited her books and grabbed her bag. She waited impatiently for Matt, who was right on time. She gave him a quick kiss, telling him she would be back by the end of the sixth period and would see him when school was out.

Mavis couldn't get out to the bus fast enough. When she arrived, she felt a bit like a worrywart: half the class wasn't even there yet, and here she was, racing around like a banshee. Ms. Randall, her psychology teacher, was standing by the bus door, with her clipboard. She was telling everyone to get in line at the door, but it seemed that no one was paying attention to a word she said. Mavis, as usual, stood at the door and waited patiently for Ms. Randall to completely lose her cool, which she did. By the time everyone was seated, and the bus was pulling away from the school, they were already five minutes behind schedule. Ms. Randall looked like she was ready to quit her job.

All the way to the hospital Mavis thought about her future. The very idea of working with children filled her with both passion and compassion; she wanted to do something that made a difference in people's lives, and this seemed like the obvious choice in her mind. She wondered what the lectures would be about, and hoped that they spent a lot of time on Child Psychology specifically. Regardless, it was going to be a great day, she was sure of it. As it turned out, not every aspect of that day was perfect.

When they first got there, Ms. Randall had them line up against the wall outside the administration offices to wait while she went inside to let the staff know they had arrived. From there, they were greeted by a tour guide, who thanked them for their interests in their chosen fields, and who bragged up the hospital's "state of the art" standing a bit. At last, the tour guide, a plump red-head named Freda, began leading them to the Psych Department, which was located on the top floor of the building for security reasons. She explained that the hospital had two psych units: One that was "open," which housed patients who didn't exhibit self-harming behaviors or try to abscond from their treatment, and another that was locked for the safety of both staff and patient. They would be allowed to tour the open unit after meeting with the lecturing staff in the conference room on the sixth floor. After that, they would be taken on a much quicker, shorter tour of the rest of the hospital, including the Greenville Morgue, which was housed in the basement.

"I'm so excited!" Kelly Jensen was standing next to Mavis, her face flushed and her eyes alight. "I have been waiting for this all year, and I thought that the psych tour was going to be the best, but the morgue too? This is going to be so cool!"

Mavis smiled at her, barely able to contain herself either. "I know. I didn't expect this to be so all-inclusive."

"It's going to be great," Kelly said in a voice barely above a whisper. "Let's get this thing started already!"

So, they did. Freda began walking slowly, pointing out things like the waiting room, gift shop, and other places that were of little consequence to their purpose as they made their way to the elevator. When they reached the elevator area, Freda stopped and briefed them on the fact that the rest of the first floor consisted of the cafeteria and administrative offices, which they wouldn't see on tour. She then told the kids that the tour would begin on the psych floor and that the remainder of the hospital and its various units would be toured on their way down, part taking place before lunch, and the remainder afterward. As the students gravitated in small groups into the elevators, Kelly Jensen stuck close to Mavis. At first, Mavis felt a bit uncomfortable; she had known Kelly practically her entire educational career. The two had never really been friends, though they had spoken in passing countless times. But once they were on the elevator and the doors closed, Kelly turned to her and smiled.

"I didn't know you were interested in psychology, Mavis." The girl's cheeks flushed slightly. "Had I known, I definitely would have spent more time with you the last couple of years; I'll bet you have some of the best insights in the senior class."

Mavis was immediately flattered. "Wow, Kelly, thanks! But I'm sure your interests and insights are just as profound and compelling."

The girl humbly shook her head and turned her attention to the front of the car, the blush still on her cheeks. "I only got interested in majoring in the subject toward the end of last summer… when a cousin of mine took a wrong turn and got into some legal trouble. It fascinated me that she could come from a loving home and still choose the wrong road. I had to ask myself, 'What is inside a person that really drives their choices, if not familial background?' You know what I mean? I guess my interest grew stronger from there. How about you?"

Mavis shrugged. "I really enjoy children. I want to

be more than a babysitter to delinquents or an adoptive parent; I want to make a difference in as many lives as I can. I guess in my opinion, the best place to start if you want to make a difference is in childhood, so child psych it is. Do you mind if I ask who your cousin is? Are they from Greenville?"

Kelly glanced over her shoulder to see who in the car might be listening. Satisfied that they were speaking privately, she answered in a whispered, embarrassed tone. Her voice was so low that Mavis, whose arm was actually touching Kelly's, had to lean forward to pick up the name.

"Candy," Kelly replied. "Candy Wilkes. Do you remember her from last year?"

Mavis almost choked on her own spit. She quickly saved face and recovered, flashing a slightly sympathetic smile and nodding. Didn't Kelly know that Mavis was caught up in the middle of not only Candy's criminal charges but also her subsequent death? As the elevator stopped, Mavis gently put her hand on Kelly's arm to hold her back as the other students filed off onto the sixth-floor Psychiatric Department.

"Kelly," she muttered into the girl's ear as they stepped off, "aren't you aware that Candy's... issues... involved me?"

Without skipping a beat, the girl nodded and offered an apologetic grin. "Yeah. I guess I should have been more straightforward. From what I know of you, from what I've observed over the years, I feel bad. I'm sorry for her behavior, Mavis."

"And I'm sorry for your loss," Mavis replied.

Freda the tour guide interrupted with her loud voice. "Okay, students, here we are, Greenville Medical's Psychiatric Services Department. Gather around so I can fill all of you in on the process of the lecture and how you are expected to behave during said lecture, please."

As Freda droned on, Mavis glanced over at Kelly, who still stood next to her, her eyes focused diligently on Freda as she listened to her words. Kelly was alright; Mavis knew that. She was a good student with goals and ambitions she was attentive to, and she never got into trouble or drew negative attention to herself. No wonder Mavis saw Kelly by herself most of the time; the girl likely got a lot of flak for being the cousin of the convicted murderer, Candace Wilkes. Poor girl; even she was convinced that Candy had been guilty, and only Mavis knew better. Her stomach gave a guilt-spurred lurch; it was the least she could do to spend the tour day with Kelly Jensen if that was what Kelly wanted.

Before she knew what was happening, Freda was directing the class to follow her, and the tour of the sixth-floor began. With a pounding heart, Mavis followed the rest of the students from the rear, with Kelly right beside her. Every now and then, the girl would look at her and laugh at something and then look at Mavis for approval. Mavis complied every time with a nod.

It was going to be a very interesting day, to say the least.

CHAPTER 10

"In conclusion: the most important thing to remember is to always use compassion. The people you will be working with are human beings with feelings and emotions."

The lecturing psychologist was speaking in a gentle, but firm, voice as he smiled and gazed over the class. "Thank you for your interest in the field, and may each and every one of you spark change in the lives of those you work with in the future; I wish you all great success."

Mavis closed the notebook in which she had been furiously jotting throughout the lecture. She felt a brand-new sense of enthusiasm regarding her career choice, and she had learned a lot from the man who had lectured, Dr. Fields. She felt more certain than ever that she had made the right decision to study this topic, and she found that she could hardly wait to start college and get on with that part of her life.

"He had so many good things to share, don't you think?"

Mavis looked over at Kelly Jensen, who was sitting next to her gathering up her own things. Kelly's eyes were as lit up as hers felt, and it made her feel good to think she wasn't the only student to get something out of the short, basic lecture he had given. She nodded and gave Kelly a smile.

"I love it," she replied as she shoved her notebook and pen in her bag. "I can hardly wait to get to college; I'm much more excited than I thought I would be."

As other students filed past them to meet Freda in the hall, Mavis got a big whiff of fresh beef; her vapor rub was wearing off! She reached into her bag and grabbed the small jar she had gotten into the habit of taking with her everywhere. As Kelly watched in stunned silence, Mavis took a glob of the gel out of the jar with her forefinger and smeared it liberally under her nose. After she had recapped the jar and replaced it in her bag, she glanced over at Kelly. Suddenly she was thoroughly embarrassed; Kelly was looking at her as if she had just grown a third arm out of her forehead.

"I have sinus problems," Mavis told her sheepishly. "This seems to be the only thing that clears it up. Does the smell bother you?"

Right away, Kelly smiled and shook her head. "Nah. I just never saw anyone use it like that before. Sorry for staring."

Mavis giggled nervously. "Well, we'd better get going, or the group is going to leave without us."

With that, the two girls jumped up and rushed off after the rest of the class to resume the tour. Mavis gave a mental sigh of relief, along with a mental head slap; that had been a close call. Usually, she was much more careful about taking her precautions, but she had been so excited about the tour, and in such a hurry, that she hadn't thought twice when she used her vapor rub. She had better be more careful in the future, that was for sure.

So, the tour continued on as the class worked their way down each consecutive floor of Greenville Medical Center. They visited the heart and lung unit, rehabilitation, the surgical floor, and the labor and delivery section, talking to doctors and nurses during each stop. After the third floor was complete, they went back down to the first-floor cafeteria to have their lunch. Kelly and Mavis sat with each other and ate slices of pizza with soda pop on ice.

During their meal the conversation was light, but Mavis could tell that Kelly was constantly on the verge of bringing something up but holding back each time she came close. Mavis also knew that it was about Candy, this subject, and she gave the girl plenty of opportunities to go ahead, but Kelly didn't seem able to cross the conversational line. Finally, Mavis decided to alleviate the tension by bringing up the topic herself during a short pause.

"You know, I don't have anything against your cousin," she began, "and to be honest, I consider her more of a victim than anything else."

Kelly looked up from her pizza, surprise all over her face. "You do?" she asked incredulously.

Mavis nodded. "I watched Shanice Hall run her around like a slave for years. When they jumped me in the alley last year, which was what started all of the problems, it was at Shanice's influence. I'm willing to bet on that. Don't blame her too much; she was under Shanice's thumb for years."

Kelly looked at her in silence for a long moment, as if she were trying to read Mavis' mind and see if she was telling the truth about her feelings. It took her several minutes to conclude that she believed Mavis. At last, the girl's face softened, and she smiled.

"You really mean that, don't you?" she asked.

Mavis nodded. "I really do."

"Thank you."

Right then, Freda called for the class to empty their trays properly in the dish line, and meet the rest of the class in the hall for the rest of the tour. Next, they would visit radiology and the lab, then they would be heading on down to the morgue. Kelly was excited; she had been looking forward to this part of the tour all day.

"I can hardly wait to get down to the morgue," Kelly was saying as they left the cafeteria and made their way to the first-floor gift shop. "I mean, I came for the psych lecture, but there's just something about dead bodies that is so intriguing if you know what I mean."

Mavis groaned inwardly; if only the girl knew. "I know exactly what you mean. It will be cool to see how they handle the bodies. I'm pretty interested as well."

The students filed into the gift shop in small groups and were allowed to purchase one item for memorabilia. They were also given small plastic bags with baseball caps with the "Greenville Medical Center" logo on them, as well as name tags that made them official Greenville employees (so to speak). Inside was also a letter of thanks from all the psych unit staff at the hospital. It was a pretty cool way of helping the students to remember that day in the future, and hopefully their goals and ambitions.

Then it was time for the basement morgue. The class made their way back to the elevators, but at the last minute, Freda decided that it would be best to take the stairway down due to the size of the class; she didn't want to hold up any employees who may be going about important business.

It was at the bottom of the stairs that Mavis began to feel a little… funny.

Freda was going on and on about how the city used the hospital instead of a separate facility to save taxpayers' money and keep all medical and post-mortem services under one roof. Her words began to fade in and out as if she were nothing more than a radio announcer, and Mavis had a bad connection or signal.

"Mavis, are you okay?" They were at the bottom of the stairs, and a blurry glance at Kelly told Mavis that the girl was concerned.

"Yeah, yeah," she replied in a slurred voice. "I'm… I'm great."

They stepped through the heavy double doors, and that was when the smell hit her: dead, rotting flesh.

"Mavis?"

She turned to Kelly one more time, her head swimming and her brain not grasping the girl's words or even who she was. Kelly had her by the arm now, and she was asking for help in a strange, faraway voice that sounded like it was coming from the far end of a tunnel. Mavis turned to her right just in time to see Freda and Ms. Randall rushing toward her with looks of alarm on their faces.

That was it. Her legs went weak, and she fell to the hard concrete floor in a dead faint and a crumpled heap while the entire class gathered around her to stare.

CHAPTER 11

Mavis woke to the feeling of being carried over to the bed and stinging smell of antiseptic in her nose. The distant sound of voices discussing muffled things that she couldn't yet comprehend. A deep craving was nagging at her from the inside, a craving for meat that seemed insatiable, and her stomach growled in an effort to torture her to insanity. Bright lights were shining down on her, hurting her eyes and her head.

"Where… where am I?"

She was surrounded by people, and a balding man in a white coat bent over her, his own eyes wide with wonder. "She's still with us! I need everyone out of here immediately, please. Get me an I.V. started and order an EKG stat."

Mavis raised her arm to block the lights and squinted to see the man better. He had a name tag on the left side of his coat that read "Dr. Martinez," and a row of pens in a protector stuck out of a pocket on the right. He was attempting to shine a penlight in her eyes, but she blocked his attempts and began to sit up.

"No, no, Miss Harvey," he said softly. "I'm going to need you to lie here quietly for a bit. We aren't quite sure of your condition. Can you tell me what happened down in the morgue earlier?"

Suddenly, it all came back to her. She had been with her psych class, and they had been getting ready to tour the morgue. The smell of the dead bodies had hit her hard, and she had become so sick to her stomach that it made her head swim; even the vapor rub hadn't been able to block it from her senses. That had been the last thing she remembered.

"I don't know; I guess the smell of the bodies was just too much for me."

The doctor clicked off the penlight and stood up straight, studying her with a slight look of confusion on his face. "Miss Harvey, we seem to have something of a… dilemma, if you will." He took his stethoscope from around his neck and started to place the earpieces in, but Mavis abruptly sat up all the way before he could stop her.

"I'm fine," she told him with a smile. "Where is my mother?"

Dr. Martinez gave her a strange look. "We thought you were dead, I need you to listen to me now. As you were brought to the ER, I checked your vitals, and it seems—"

Mavis held up her hand to stop him and smiled. "I know, I know. You couldn't find my heartbeat or pulse. I get that a lot. It just takes a little more work than usual, that's all. But as you can see, I'm alive and well!" She jumped down from the exam table as her stomach gave yet another loud growl. "As a matter of fact, I'm starved, and to be honest, I'm ready to go home and be done with this day."

As if on cue, Jane entered the exam room with a look of near-panic on her face. "Mavis! My my, what happened?"

The doctor was utterly confused, and his face showed it clearly. "I think you should stay for some tests, young lady."

Mavis smiled and headed to her bag, which she spotted on the floor, leaning against the wall next to a chair. "I'm fine, Mom. I smelled the bodies in the morgue, and they made me sick; I guess I passed out. But I'm fine now. Let's go."

"Wait, Mrs. Harvey." Dr. Martinez' voice was firm and tinged slightly with frustration. "I was unable to detect a heartbeat or pulse when examining your daughter. I believe her heart stopped on the way to the ER; it is in her best interest to stay over for at least a night, or until I am able to determine normalcy. She was ice cold, and for all intents and purposes, I thought she was dead."

Jane turned to the doctor and looked at him as though he had lost his mind. "Dead? Can't you see her standing there, holding a conversation with us and gathering her things?"

"Ma'am, I'm quite serious," he persisted. "I couldn't detect her vitals, we need to monitor her."

Jane rolled her eyes and shook her head. "Are you sure you feel okay, dear?"

Mavis nodded and put her bag over her shoulder.

"Just starving, that's all."

"Well, Dr. Martinez, I would say that's a pretty good sign." Jane put her arm protectively over Mavis' shoulders. "We'll be leaving now; my daughter needs to eat."

Mavis smiled at the doctor as they left the room. "Thanks for the help, but I'll be okay."

Before he could respond, they left and let the door swing shut behind them. Ms. Randall stood in the hall looking frazzled. Mavis stopped to reassure her that she was in tip-top shape, but that she would be going home to rest for the day; then she and her mother left the hospital. She braced herself for all kinds of questions about the incident in the morgue, and especially the situation with her vitals.

But her mother was silent until they got into the car and fastened their safety belts. Mavis placed her bag on the floorboard and set about latching hers. Jane dropped her purse onto the console and clicked hers together, then immediately turned to her daughter and stared at her without even attempting to start the ignition. Mavis could feel her gaze and turned to Jane with false wonder in her eyes.

"What, Mom?"

Jane paused. "Are you sure you're feeling okay?" she asked.

Mavis nodded, then looked forward and waited for Jane to start the car, but her mother did nothing but continue to stare. Mavis looked back at her for a moment. What was she doing, just sitting there like that?

"Well, are we going?" she asked.

"What did that doctor mean, no vital signs?" Jane's voice was low and tinged with both worry and suspicion. "You know, that would explain a lot of things, even though it makes no sense whatsoever that you are walking and talking."

Mavis sat there, stumped as to what to say, keeping her eyes straight ahead. After a minute, she gave a light chuckle and turned to Jane. "Mom, that guy is crazy! There is no possible way that could be! I mean, here I am, sitting next to you talking, and you are curious about his whacked out theory?"

Another pause. "We are going to go home and talk about this, Mavis Jean. I have been having some pretty weird thoughts about your condition from day one, and now I think it's time to explore those thoughts further."

With that, Jane started the car and threw it into reverse, then backed out and aimed the vehicle for home. Mavis' stomach trembled nervously inside; it looked like this might be it, this might be the outing of Mavis, the zombie. How she wished Matt was with her right now! But maybe it was better to face it alone, just her and her mother. Maybe that was the only way to really do it.

She stared straight ahead as Jane drove, and they made the trip home in complete silence.

∞

Jane sat across from her daughter at the kitchen

table with a cup of steaming coffee in front of her. Mavis had a plate of food, but she hadn't touched it yet; it smelled repulsive. She wished she could get to that cow heart in the cooler in her room but now was definitely not the time. Her mother was staring at her with a scrutinizing look, waiting patiently for her daughter to eat, and knowing that the girl would not. Unbeknownst to Mavis, Jane had been harboring some fairly odd suspicions regarding her daughter's condition, her anemia condition, for quite some time. There was an unsettling amount of details she had taken in, which caused her to question the entire situation. But as a loving mother, who was also her daughter's best friend, she had simply gone with the flow since it had all begun.

But today was different. The doctor at Greenville Medical had been very specific about his concerns, citing symptoms which Jane felt confirmed the suspicions she had all along. There would be no more waiting to broach the subject. She wouldn't wait for Todd or allow Matt or Kim to be involved. She planned to confront Mavis right there at the kitchen table, while it was just the two of them and honesty would be all that passed across the table.

She studied her daughter a moment longer; Mavis stared nervously down at her plate, fidgeting a bit in her chair. She was so pale, and Jane knew that was a major part of what was going on. The Goth style she had taken to was also a sure sign, especially considering when she began to don it. She practically force-fed her meals to herself; Jane had only been pretending not to notice that for the last year. Then she would retreat to her room where, behind closed doors, she would eat something sounding like a wild animal tearing into its prey.

Now was the time that Mavis would let the cat out of the bag.

Mavis, on the other hand, had no appetite for the food before her whatsoever. She began to pick slightly at the food, feeling her mother's stare the entire time. She took tiny bites and made sure she chewed each into mush before allowing it to slide down her throat. After about ten minutes of this, she was interrupted by Jane abruptly.

"Put the fork down, Mavis, and stop faking it," she said firmly. "It's time we had a talk. I know what's going on, and believe it or not, I don't care. But I need to hear it from you. I need you to tell me the truth, finally, after all this time."

Mavis gulped down her small bite and made eye contact with Jane, who looked very determined. Here it was, the thing she had been dreading. She could tell by the sound of her mom's voice that she knew more than Mavis ever suspected.

She took a deep breath and braced herself as she commenced, to tell the truth to Jane.

R.W.K. Clark

CHAPTER 12

"Well, it all started last fall, in my junior year," Mavis began. "When I got sick, and the doctor said I had anemia."

Jane's facial expression remained stony, her eyes focused entirely on those of her daughter, who was more than a bit nervous. She waited for a brief moment for Mavis to go on, then lost her patience. Jane was ready to get down to the real nitty-gritty, alright.

"And?"

Mavis took another deep breath and began to tear her napkin into tiny little bits. "Well, at first I was just starving all the time, and nothing seemed to fill me up. And not only that, I was having cravings for the strangest things."

"Like what?" Jane asked in a flat tone.

Mavis felt like she was going to be sick; how could she possibly brooch this subject honestly without giving her mother a heart attack? All she knew was that she loved Jane very, very much. The thought of lying to her now after she had asked directly about what was going on, Mavis just knew she had to be honest. She just had no idea how, and she was more than petrified at what

Jane's reaction was going to be to the outlandish truth she was about to divulge.

Clearing her throat and bucking up her courage, Mavis finally met her mother's eyes and said boldly, "Raw flesh."

She had braced herself for the complete ungluing of her mother. She had thought of every possible scenario that could take place when this moment finally came for the last year and a half, but Jane's true reaction wasn't one of those at all. Instead, the woman sat back in her chair, crossed her arms, and studied her daughter in silence. The serious look on her face was intent on determining if her daughter was yanking her chain or not. Finally, after several minutes, she sat forward and asked a single question.

"What does this have to do with the fact that the doctor at the ER said you have no vitals, Mavis Jean?"

Mavis' hands were beginning to tremble, and she began to tear at the napkin even more intently. "I should tell you that, at first, I had no idea what was going on myself. I ate what you fed me so you wouldn't worry, but I went through a long period of eating raw liver that I bought at Flair's, and I snuck a few other raw things from the freezer just to get by. There were also a few... incidents that I indulged in that are less than appropriate for casual conversation."

"I would hardly call this 'casual conversation,' young lady." Jane's voice was getting a bit more stern, and it was tinged with frustration.

Mavis put her forehead down on the top of her

hands on the table. "This is so hard, Mom."

Suddenly, Jane reached forward and put her hand on top of Mavis' head. "Honey, there is nothing you can tell me that will make me love you less, I swear to you."

Looking up, Mavis replied, "I'm pretty sure this will."

Jane continued to stare and wait.

With a groan, Mavis finally spoke, spilling it out all at once and letting the chips fall where they may.

"Mom, in the beginning, when I first got sick, and until Matt helped me understand what was happening to me and helped me find ways to live with it. I was eating people, specifically, my dates."

Jane's mouth fell open immediately, and her eyes took on the look of either madness or extreme disbelief. She appeared ready to crack up laughing, or perhaps she was going to cry, Mavis couldn't tell. All she knew was that she felt her life falling apart right before her very eyes.

It was laughter that Jane opted for, but it sounded like the laughter of someone who had just been the victim of a practical joke. When the laughter died down, she studied Mavis, terrified for a few brief moments. She shook her head, tears welling up in her eyes and said, "I suppose you are telling me that you are the one who ate Jeff Deason and Colin Handley, right? And what about Detective Gordon, Mavis? Did you eat him too? And all those others?"

"No, Mother, not Uncle Ben" she replied, on the verge of tears. "By then, we had it figured out and had things under control. Yes, Jeff and Colin, but they were accidents before I met Matt and he helped me."

Jane glanced up at the clock and grabbed her cell. Without a word, she began tapping away at the screen, her hands shaking uncontrollably and soon Mavis could hear the faded sound of ringing on the other end. She heard the other party pick up.

Jane was calling Matt; "Matthew, are you out of class yet?" She paused while he answered. "Well, don't wait for Mavis any longer; she's here with me. I know you have to work, but this is a family emergency, and I need you to come over here right away, as soon as humanly possible please." Another pause. "Fine, thank you; see you soon."

Jane hung up and looked at Mavis. "He's on his way. We will not discuss this further until he arrives. Why don't you go to your room? I need to think, Mavis Jean Harvey."

Without a word, the girl rose and went to her room, where she collapsed face-first onto her bed and cried tearless sobs for the next fifteen minutes. It was hopeless. It had all come to a head, and now it was all going to fall apart. She was scared to death and wished that Matt would hurry.

CHAPTER 13

Shanice Hall was lounging on the deck of her yacht, waiting for her stud, Brad, the tanned and blonde slave she enjoyed torturing, to bring her favorite icy cocktail. Her eyes were closed beneath her sunglasses, and she was smiling as she thought about dinner.

"Here you are, my beautiful butterfly."

Shanice opened her eyes to see Brad leaning over her, his tan glaringly dark, set off by his white Speedos. He had a sparkling smile on his face, and in his hand, he held a tray which toted a frothy blue and pink creation with a swizzle stick poking out of the top. Lately, he had been studying a variety of cocktails online so that he could surprise her with each and every drink. Shanice always acted impressed, but the fact of the matter was that she would have been satisfied with anything. It amused her that he tried so hard, regardless, and she thanked him with a smooth, flirty voice.

"You should probably get ready to hunt for dinner," she suggested.

"Fine. I'm heading inland, then, to track down some new, tasty flavors. Do you have a preference tonight?"

"Hmmm." Shanice thought about it, but it only took

her a moment. "I think I'm craving Italian, zesty perhaps, yes, I would like dark meat tonight. You find whatever suits you. See you when you get back, but hurry and leave. I need to be alone for my calls and research."

Shanice calmly sipped at her drink, enjoying the fresh fruity flavor, but not really focusing on it. She was too busy listening for the sound of Brad leaving for shore in the small boat. Once he was gone, she would be able to go about her business. Sometimes he was worse than a woman when it came to getting ready. She didn't let herself indulge in impatience, and soon enough, she heard the boat, and she watched him disappear across the water toward shore.

This time, however, her selfishness caused her to miss some hints that Brad gave about his plans for "shopping," and they would have infuriated her.

Had she not been so wrapped up in herself, Shanice would have taken care of his defiance ahead of time.

∞

By 4:30 that same afternoon, Matthew Morgan had joined Mavis and her mother at the Harvey dining room table. At this point, Jane was beside herself with both concern and disbelief, and she was more than anxious to hear Matt's version of the story that Mavis was trying to feed her. More than anything else, she wanted this cleared up before her husband Todd returned home from work. After all, as his wife, she was responsible for telling him all that had been going on with his family and under his roof while he was away. If what Mavis was saying had even a shred of truth to it, Jane simply didn't know where to begin.

So, once she had Matt settled in a chair with a cold soda in front of him, she shut Mavis out and turned her attention to the young man she had grown to love as a son. She trusted him and knew that he wouldn't blow smoke. If what Mavis was saying was true, though she didn't yet have the rest of the details, Matt would confirm it. Once he was comfortable, she filled him in on what happened at Greenville Medical, what the ER doctor had said, and told him the small bit of information Mavis had offered. She also watched Matt's skin turn pale at the admissions and glance at his girlfriend frequently, which was confirmation enough for Jane. Finally, she demanded his version of the story in full, and she also instructed him not to lie, or he would lose her trust forever. He had also better leave nothing out, no matter how graphic or difficult to take. Her final command was that Mavis utter not so much as a peep. She already had a very good idea what her daughter was attempting to insinuate, and she wanted to hear how close Matt's story resembled hers.

"Okay, Matthew," she said, dread filling her stomach at the thought of something so far-fetched being the truth. "Let's hear it, and no looking at each other for help."

Matt was so calm that Mavis admired him more than ever. Just as she imagined, he began to talk directly to Jane in a very matter-of-fact manner that exuded calm confidence. Why shouldn't he be calm? He was telling the truth, and he knew it; that's just how Matt was.

"You know, Mrs. Harvey, I'm really glad this finally happened." He sat back in his chair and crossed his arms over his chest, looking her in the eye. "This has really been a major burden for us to carry around and keep quiet, but particularly for Mavis. The guilt she has been living with has kept her in a state of confusion for more than a year."

Jane gave a sarcastic eye-roll and stood up with her coffee cup to refill it. "You mean the secret of eating raw meat, right?" She turned and proceeded to walk towards the kitchen.

Matt kept his eyes on her, regardless. "Not just eat it, but crave it to the point of loss of control. And not just any raw meat, but human meat."

Suddenly, in only a fraction of a second, after he stopped dead in his tracks with his words, Jane's empty coffee cup slipped from her hand and smashed to the floor in shards great and small. She just stood there, frozen, her back still to the kids. Both of them exchanged concerned glances; was Jane having a heart attack?

They gave her a moment since she was still standing upright and not grabbing her chest or anything. But she stood like that for some time before Mavis was unable to control herself any longer. Bracing herself, she took a deep breath.

"Um… Mom? Are you okay?"

Jane's arm still bent at the elbow from holding the

coffee cup, flinched slightly and then dropped to her side as if all the strength had drained from it. Slowly, she turned and looked first at her daughter, then at Matt. Jane studied them both for several minutes while they stared back at her in silence. It was best to let her process right then, they both knew.

Then it was Jane's turn to cross her arms over her chest, and suddenly a broad grin came over her mouth. "Basically, kids, what I hear you are telling me is that Mavis drank sludge water about eighteen months ago and it has turned her into a flesh-eating zombie. That she has been covering up, though not with complete success, ever since."

Both Matt and Mavis nodded, careful to maintain their stillness and serious façade.

With the broken cup long forgotten, Jane began to make her way to her chair, her hand reaching out for it blindly as her mind raced. She began to chuckle a bit, then, and soon she was crying and barely able to get herself sat down. Matt quickly rose to help her and get her securely seated.

Jane continued to laugh and cry for some time while the kids traded frequent nervous looks. Slowly, but surely, the laughter began to subside, ebbing away in the same manner in which it had bloomed. She wiped her tearing eyes with her shirt sleeve, chuckled a bit more, then looked at Mavis, her grimace still in place.

"So, you want to eat humans, but you eat raw liver to keep yourself from doing that, huh?" she asked.

Matt took the liberty to answer. "Well, only if she

has to now. Since I started at the packing house, I have been providing her with fresh scraps on a daily basis. You know, hearts and kidneys and brains and things. Seems to keep her satisfied."

Jane's eyes flashed to Matt and gave him a quick glare, as if to say, "I don't believe you." She then turned her eyes back to her daughter and asked, "So, you have eaten human meat, Mav?"

The trepidation in her voice was thick, and she was primed for more, Mavis could tell. She didn't have to glance at Matt to know what she should say to that question: she had to tell the truth. There was no other way to take care of the issue and get rid of the secrets once and for all. Besides, who did she trust more in the world than her mother?

"Mom," she said slowly, her eyes wary and a bit frightened, "the answer to that is yes."

Immediately, Jane's mouth flew open, and her hand shot up to cover it. With wide eyes, she stared at her daughter in disbelief, but something in them told Mavis she believed her fully. It was almost as if Mavis could see the pieces of the puzzle coming together in her mother's mind all by themselves.

"Mavis," she whispered at last, tears forming in her eyes, "I know earlier you said you were eating people and your boyfriends, but I guess it just didn't register with me, don't tell me…"

"Yes, Mother. I'm so sorry." She looked down at the table in shame and fear. "I ate my boyfriends."

In a fraction of a second, Jane's eyes began to flutter, she slid off her chair and hit the floor in a dead faint.

R.W.K. Clark

CHAPTER 14

"She's coming around now; I knew she'd be okay. It was just a faint, that's all."

Jane was lying comfortably on the sofa in the family room, a cold, wet washcloth folded neatly across her forehead. Matt had carried the woman in there, with Mavis having a firm hold on her feet. Together, they had managed to get her off the floor and onto the couch so they could bring her back to reality if it were at all possible. Now, Jane's eyes were fluttering, and she looked a bit confused.

As soon as she focused on Mavis' face, it all came back to her in a rush. She shot up into a sitting position, the wet cloth falling to her lap. Staring at her daughter, her mind continued to remember what the kids had told her in the kitchen, and she knew it to be true. Now she wanted to know everything, but she wasn't sure if she could handle it right then.

"All I have to say, Mavis Jean, is I believe you." Jane glanced up at the clock hanging on the wall over the couch. "Your father will be home within twenty minutes, and we all need to talk… together. Right now, I have a headache, and I need to pee. Let me up so I can go to the bathroom. You two better ready yourselves for Todd."

Jane stood up with the washcloth in her hand and made her way to her master bathroom. Mavis and Matt watched her walk until she rounded the corner through the bedroom door, then they turned to each other looking both scared and sheepish.

"We haven't even told her the very least of the details," Mavis whispered. "She is in no way prepared to hear all the gory stuff; I mean, it's horrible."

Matt glanced toward her room briefly. "How do you think your dad will handle the news?"

Mavis thought about it for a second then shrugged. "I think he'll be like mom was at first; thinking it's a prank. But once we show them the proof, like my lack of vitals, and we tell them about Jeff and Colin, he'll believe it. He won't faint. And if I know my dad, he'll protect me at all cost."

Matt nodded. "That's the same thing I was thinking; he's so easy going and all."

As if on cue, the front door opened and Todd walked in, whistling while he put his briefcase under the foyer table and hung his jacket in the closet. He was still whistling and loosening his tie when he turned and saw the kids staring at him in silence, morose looks on their faces. The whistling stopped right away.

"What's going on?"

The kids looked at one another, then shifted their gaze back to Todd. "Mom says we need to have a family meeting… that it's really important."

"Right this very second?" he asked. "For Pete's sake, I just walked in the door. For crying out loud, I swear this happens every single day as soon as I get home. Where is your mother?"

Matt and Mavis pointed to the master bedroom in unison and kept their mouths closed.

"Jane!" Todd made his way to the bedroom and disappeared inside just as his wife had only minutes before. The kids sat back on the sofa and let out long sighs. Jane would fill him in as best as she could, then the two of them would come out and have a good old Harvey family sit down. Mavis had a feeling it may be the longest one of her life. In the meantime, they would both peel their ears and try to figure out what was being said in the bedroom.

All they could make out was muffled mumbling and an occasional "What?" Or an "Oh, that's baloney; they're pulling your leg, Jane." Finally, Todd's voice rose to a fever pitch, and he stated, with disbelief, "Oh, my! Not our sweet daughter!"

Well, Jane had managed to lay it on the line. The kids both sat up straight, adjusting their posture and making sure they had calm looks on their faces. Sure enough, Jane and Todd came out of the bedroom with long strides. Jane's face was tear-streaked, and Todd's was stricken with near-panic. Taking their favorite chairs, both of the Harvey parents faced the kids, but it was Todd who spoke first, and he spoke directly to his daughter.

"I'd say it's time for you to start at the very

beginning," he said firmly. "And it's in your best interest not to leave out a single detail. Remember, Mavis, you can trust us with anything."

Mavis gave a sigh of relief because if there was anything that she believed with her whole heart, it was the fact that she could trust her parents.

Mavis did precisely as her father requested, or demanded, anyway. She started at the beginning, with the sludgy water, the flu-like sickness, and the doctor's goofy diagnosis of anemia. Next, with much tears and apprehension, she began to fill them in on how the cravings grew and grew, how she sated them with raw liver from Flair Foods, and how she eventually ended up accidentally eating Jeff Deason. She also covered the details about Colin Handley and the prom night massacre, making sure they understood how frightened and sickened she was by her own behavior. Matt explained that, until he came around and figured things out, Mavis was living in a state of horrible confusion and was crippled with guilt, even after Candy Wilkes was incarcerated. Finally, they told about how she had bitten Shanice Hall, and now Shanice was a zombie, too.

By the time they had finished, with no stone left unturned, both kids could tell that Jane and Todd still had significant doubts. That was when Matt made the decision to show them what the ER doctor had been trying to tell Jane that afternoon: Mavis had no vital signs that were in any way detectable. He excused himself and went to his bag, which was in Mavis' room. There, he fished out his stethoscope, thermometer, and pen light and returned to his seat next to Mavis.

"Well, here is the final proof." He held up the three items awkwardly and looked at both of the adults. "First, we'll take her temperature. While we wait for that, both of you can take turns trying to find her heartbeat, and finally, I will show you that her pupils no longer dilate or shrink."

They went through the process, with initial doubts, but by the time they were finished, both were stunned and had no words. The pair simply stared at each other for a long time, looks of pain and fear on their faces. It was Todd who broke the silence.

"Besides the meat from the pack, how do you keep from losing control around people, Mav?" he asked.

Embarrassed, she replied, "I smear vapor rub under my nose all the time, and use a lot of perfume."

Todd raised his eyebrows, impressed. "Nice," he said. Then his face got very serious. "Matt, I appreciate your help today, but I think you should head home, so you're not late for work. Jane and I have some pretty serious things to discuss. Mavis needs to wait, alone, in her room for us and think about why she should have come to us in the very beginning."

Todd looked down at his hands.

Matt gave Mavis a peck on the cheek before he rose, grabbed his bag, and left, promising to call her. Todd and Jane just stared at Mavis until she came to her senses and stood to go to her room. She paused at the mouth of the hallway.

"I love you guys?"

They both answered in unison, "We love you too."

With that, Mavis made her way down the hall and shut herself in her room so her parents could figure out what all of this meant to their future as a family.

CHAPTER 15

Shanice's cell phone chirped annoyingly. Immediately, Shanice rose and fetched her cell phone from her bag. She quickly answered on the first ring. A glance down at the screen told her that the call was from another one of her lackeys: Sonny Maneli, PI. Good, she thought as she answered the phone, another update, and hopefully, it was a good one.

"Hello, it's Miss Hall," she replied.

"So, I have a little bit to discuss about my findings today."

Shanice smiled to herself, realizing that he was stumbling over her name. She had never given him her proper moniker, and she didn't intend to.

"Tell me everything, Sonny. It's vital that you leave nothing out if this mission is to be a success."

"What have you got?" she greeted him, her voice condescending and bored-sounding.

Sonny snorted. "More than yesterday, but not as much as tomorrow, I think you'll be interested."

"I'm listening."

He cleared his throat. "Well, the first thing this morning I followed the girl and boy to school... same old, same old; same as all week no big deal. Except that Mavis had gone on the yearly senior psych trip and had passed out in the morgue."

"What?" Shanice gushed. What had the bimbo expected? The smell of rotten meat was twice as harsh to a zombie than to others, causing instant nausea and vertigo. But that wasn't the best of it.

Sonny continued, "Yes, but wait, it gets better." He replied, then he continued. "Anyway, when they went on the field trip, I wore a doctor's coat and managed to make myself present the entire time, every place they went. It was pretty boring at first: lectures and trivial information nobody cares about. Then they went down to the morgue. That's when it happened."

He had Shanice's full attention now.

"The girl got one whiff of the corpses down there and passed out cold; ended up in the ER."

"Then what? What happened?"

"Well, I lingered outside her ER room door long enough to catch the doctor saying that he couldn't detect her vitals, he thought she was dead."

He chuckled smugly at the recollection. "While I was posted outside the door of her room with a fake clipboard, her mother ran by me. I heard the doctor tell her mother that her heart had stopped, she had no vitals on the way to the ER… they need to monitor her. Isn't that crazy? She died and came back, I thought I was out of a job there for a minute, haha."

Now Shanice was deep in thought; it sounded like Mavis might be on the verge of being discovered.

"What happened next?"

"Her mother dragged her out of there and took her home," he continued. Sonny sounded very pleased with himself.

Sonny continued to go on and on, but right after the first sentence, Shanice went to another place in her head. This was great! Soon, all of Toledo and Greenville would know what Mavis was, and they would be dissecting the little vixen in a lab somewhere. Then she could return and make all of the city her own. Her own army of monsters, belonging only to her, and doing only her bidding. In a distant voice, Shanice said, "Fine, we will talk again soon. Have a good one."

With that, she abruptly hung up, leaving Sonny staring dumbly at his own cell.

"Cold little…" he mumbled to himself as he tossed the cell on the sofa beside him. The fact of the matter was that he was doing a good job, and he knew it. Sure, he might not be privy to all the details of the case or have the foggiest idea why she had him on the Harvey girl's tail, but the size of the dollar signs said it all. It was something big, and before this case was over, he was going to find out exactly what it was.

Then he was going to indulge in a bit of blackmail that would finally level out the field that he was on with the snobby Miss Hall.

∞

After she disconnected from the little cockroach Sonny, Shanice was ecstatic. Oh, it couldn't be more perfect. Soon, this would all come to a head. Maybe she wouldn't even have to deal with putting the little vixen out of her misery; maybe she would become a guinea pig prisoner in some lab at the Mayo Clinic or something, and Shanice could go on with her life the way she wanted to.

It had been very good news indeed. Eventually, Shanice Hall would take over the world.

"Brad, I have a few things to do regarding our target. Mr. Maneli called with some very good news today, and I need to do some research to make sure he is completely honest. If what he has to say is true, we may be ready sooner than we initially believed."

"What was the news?" Brad asked, his eyes sparkling with excitement.

Shanice waved her forefinger back and forth to chastise his curiosity. "Now, Bradley, you know I'll fill you in when I am good and ready. You never need any more information than what is required in the here and now."

His smile faded, and he rolled his eyes.

"Now, let's eat."

∞

Shanice Hall stepped out of the shower on the yacht; wrapping one towel securely around her slender figure and another in a turban fashion on her head. With a sigh of pleasure, she walked to the mirror and wiped the steam from its surface, then leaned in close to get a look at her complexion. She certainly was pale; all the sun in the world wasn't helping. If anything, it was making matters worse. Those pesky flaky gray spots seemed to be multiplying day by day.

She stuck out her tongue at herself and turned away to get dressed. Her mind turned to the wonderful meal Brad had brought them that evening: a tall, chocolate skinned young man and his girlfriend, a gorgeous Latina. They had wonderful natural seasoning, and Shanice's mouth watered just recalling the bloody meal. She only wished Brad were so competent every evening. Usually, he brought back the cream of the crop when it came to the women he ingested, but more often than not, Shanice had to settle for the goofy looking tag-a-long who hadn't showered in days.

Once Shanice had donned her bikini and had touched up her face with a light, but effective, makeup, she began to blow dry her hair. She then pulled a thin robe over her shoulders and went out to find Brad. They both always showered after eating, due to the incredibly bloody mess they made. Since he took unbelievably long showers, she assumed that was where he was. But she soon found that his room and bathroom were empty, so she went to the deck to find him; he wasn't there either.

In the galley, however, she found he had cleaned up the mess wonderfully and was pleased. That was the best thing about him: the former cabana boy was a good worker, which was his sole purpose to her anyway; she had no intention of letting him have a "hands-on" part in Mavis' demise. She shook her thoughts out of her head and focused on the here and now. Just as she was preparing to go back up to the deck, Shanice saw a note sitting on the bar in the kitchen area.

"Shanice,

I'm going back to shore for the evening. Leftovers are in the freezer, as usual. I'm bored stiff with this routine, and to be honest, I feel like doing a little partying. Sorry, I didn't ask, but you would have said no, and I didn't invite you to come along for the same reason. Maybe you should think about getting that stick out of your rear and loosening up a little. This is going to be a horrible way to spend your immortality if you get my drift.

I'll be back by morning.

Brad"

With a loud, furious growl, Shanice crumpled the sheet of paper and threw it across the room. She closed her eyes and let out a shrill scream that, if heard, would have scared anyone half to death. She felt like a trapped animal when it came to the servants she had chosen thus far; how dare he decide to do anything without her okay? The fact was that she needed full obedience, and she didn't want to hear any complaining about it, either.

Finally, she began to calm herself, to slow her breathing and clear her head. He would be back; he had no place else to go, no one else to turn to. She would be sweet, almost syrupy, and accept him with open arms of forgiveness after giving him a soft talking to.

Then she would crush his head, feed him to the sharks, and move on to the next one.

CHAPTER 16

While Shanice was pacing around her massive yacht and planning her lackey Brad's demise, Mavis and her parents were still in their marathon family meeting regarding her "zombie-hood." They were on the last leg of the get-together, which had not only gone far better than Mavis could have hoped. It bonded her to her parents in a way she never imagined possible.

While the topic was obviously overwhelming for her folks, their love for her trumped it by leaps and bounds. It was definitely hard for them to stomach the truth about her eating not only Jeff and Colin but most of her own class as well. But it wasn't even that truth that threw them off; it was the fact that she never came to them with her condition, and she lied several times in an effort to spare their feelings, as well as her own freedom.

"I just can't believe you didn't trust us enough to take refuge in the protection and love we have always given you so freely," Todd had told her. "I mean, what did you think we would do, Mavis? Take you to the police? Or worse yet, some mad scientist who would lock you up and study you forever?"

Mavis had shrugged and looked down at her hands, ashamed of her dishonesty. "I guess I thought you might not love me, or that the truth would be more than you could bear. I was also worried you would try to take me to some doctor, and he would take me to scientists. I don't know! I just had so many outcomes in my head that I was unwilling to take the risk."

For most of their meeting, Jane had been silent, only nodding in agreement now and then, or shaking her head to signify the opposite. When she did speak, it was to ask a simple question about being a zombie or to label an emotion she felt as it related to the topic at hand. But now Jane said more than she had said the entire evening.

"Mavis, I have so much in my mind to convey, but I just don't quite know how to articulate it all," she began. "So, I guess I'm just going to start and do the best I can, sort of let the chips fall where they may. First of all, I love you with all of my heart; I would give my life to ensure that you are safe and all of your needs are met. I am your mother, but more than that, I feel as though we are good friends. That is why the fact that you didn't come to me, or to your father, hurts so much. Yes, this is a very confusing and heavy situation, but our love for you is the same as it ever has been."

Todd gave a vigorous nod, and Jane continued while Mavis waited and listened patiently, out of both love and respect.

"Well, that part is behind us now; the secrets, I mean." Jane fiddled with a wadded-up tissue that looked as though it was nearly worn through. "And now we have the truth to face and deal with… together. Which is exactly what we are going to do. The first thing we need to talk about is your diet. From what I understand, you need to have fresh meat. Matt has been taking care of this, I understand. But how does the food he brings from the pack suffice if it is not from… humans?" Jane winced slightly when she said the word "humans," and it made Mavis smile slightly with amusement.

"I'm not sure," Mavis replied. "Don't get me wrong; I crave human meat more than anything, and the lure of the scent can be overwhelming, as Jeff and Colin and the rest prove. So, I use an abundance of vapor rub, and the meat Matt brings seems to tide me over, and that's how I've been living."

Jane and Todd looked at each other, shaking their heads and smiling. "This has to be the craziest thing I have ever heard of, much less dealt with," Todd said to his wife. Shifting his eyes to Mavis, he asked, "So, just to confirm, the gist of all this is that you are, for all intents and purposes, dead. And the only thing that keeps you here with us is the eating of the meat?"

Mavis grimaced and nodded. "Yes, according to Matt… and the books we've read… and TV. It seems to be what is working, anyway. According to all those things, and it's the only point they all agree on, is that without meat, I will… expire."

The smiles faded quickly from the faces of her parents, and somber looks replaced them. "So, we keep you fed, one way or another, no matter what the cost.

This is something your father and I will need to discuss in great detail. In the meantime, if it is human meat you crave, then I believe you are not getting the essential nutrients you need when you are eating cow and pig remains. Todd, what can we do about this?"

Todd flashed his wife a stern look. "Like you said, dear, this is something we will discuss alone, while we are wearing our parenting hats. Not in front of Mavis; at least, not right now."

A funny feeling filled Mavis' stomach. Was it her imagination, or were they giving silent signals to each other somehow? It seemed to her that they were mentally discussing something that she wasn't catching, and it made her uncomfortable. Before she could bring it up, however, Jane continued the conversation, taking it in another direction.

"So, from here on out, we will have nothing but honesty," she said. "We will protect and support you and this situation at all costs. I firmly believe that the good person you are is not willing to hurt anyone, and the harm that has been caused was out of your control. Only Matthew, Kim, and the three of us are aware of the situation, correct?"

Mavis shook her head. "Shanice Hall does as well; she is a zombie too. And she is planning to end me somehow; I just don't know how or when. I don't even know where she is. All I can tell you is that after Shawn was killed, she told me it wasn't the end. I believe that wherever she is, she fully intends to come back when she has all of her eggs in one basket."

Todd groaned and put his head in his hands. "Shanice… I forgot about her. And she is the one who killed Ben Gordon." He looked at his wife again. "What are we going to do about this girl, Jane?"

Jane had a faraway look in her eyes that was tinged with anger. "I don't know, but the two of us are going to figure something out. No rotten little girl like Shanice Hall is going to ruin our daughter, I can promise you that."

"I think we're done here, for now, Mavis," Todd said firmly, but with a gentle smile on his face. "So, we understand that honesty is the only acceptable way to deal with anything. We are on your side all the time, even in the most challenging of situations. There is never a reason to lie or withhold the truth from either one of us. Got it?"

"Got it," she replied. "I'm sorry for not coming to you, and I can promise you that it will never happen again."

Her parents stood up. "We have a lot to talk about, your dad and I," Jane said. "So, if you'll excuse us, I'm sure you'd like to get some sleep. Or… do you sleep?"

Mavis grinned. "Well, I do, but I'm not convinced it's necessary. I think it just feels good, so it's sort of easy."

"Well, are you hungry then? I don't have any cow parts except for some liver, and I'd have to thaw it in the microwave."

Mavis made a face. "That would ruin it. Besides, I have some leftovers in the cooler in my room."

"Oh, my," Jane groaned. "New rule: no animal innards in coolers in your room. I'll clean out the bottom shelf of the fridge for you in the morning." She looked at Todd and smiled. "This would be so difficult if we had other kids, wouldn't it?"

"I don't even want to think about it," he mumbled.

With that, Jane and Todd went to their room, and Mavis retired to the table with her own plate, knife, fork, and plenty of napkins. It would be a relief to eat properly; no more garbage bags covering the floor. No more rushing to clean up before school.

Her parents were right: honesty was the best policy.

CHAPTER 17

Shanice was sitting in her favorite lounger, sipping a mimosa and waiting for Brad's return. The sun was just on the rise, telling her that her traitorous minion should be arriving soon, so she fixed her drink and took to her seat to wait for his arrival. It wasn't a long wait. She heard the boat approaching before she could even see it, so she calmly sat and sipped, waiting to see his head pop up over the rail as he climbed the ladder to the deck on the yacht. The next ten minutes or so would be interesting, she knew full well.

Continuing to slowly sip on her mimosa, she smiled as she heard him tie up the small boat. She could hear his footsteps, though she could tell that he was much more stealthy than usual. Typically, Brad was something of a very handsome oaf, making noise no matter what it was he was doing, but now it was as though a small child were approaching. Yes, he was nervous about having to speak with her, that much was certain.

Then he reached the top, and instead of immediately climbing over the railing and onto the deck, he stopped just at the railing and looked around. It was only seconds before his eyes met hers, and for a fraction of a second, panic crossed his face. But she had to hand it to the idiot: he regained his composure immediately and began to smile at her, a flashy, happy smile that betrayed his true feelings of dread.

"Did you have fun last night, Love?" she asked sweetly.

Brad maintained his smile, but from where she sat she could see him breathe a sigh of relief as if he suddenly believed he was in the clear because of her pleasantry. He hoisted himself over the gap in the railing and onto the deck, then he stopped long enough to take a deep breath and run his hands through his hair.

"It was nothing special," he replied nonchalantly. "A bit of drinking and partying is all. I hope you weren't too angry about my decision to go; I just needed a change of scenery."

Swinging her feet to the deck surface, she drained her mimosa and placed the glass gently on the small side table. Turning to him, Shanice stood and smiled, then slowly began to stride toward him, a soft, accepting look on her face. But Brad's smile faltered, and she knew right away that he suspected what was coming.

"Well, I'm glad you were able to have the break from me that you thought you needed," she said as she reached out and ran her fingers through his hair. He flinched, and that angered her, but she kept it in check for a moment longer. "Now that you are well-rested, I can put you out of your misery."

In a flash, she grabbed his long mane of hair and yanked hard, and with a knife in the other removed his very head from his neck. Black goo shot from the torn, gaping hole, shooting toward the sky and splattering on the deck. She took no notice of the mess; she was completely entranced by the scene before her. As Shanice stood, Brad's wide-eyed head dangling from her right hand, his body jerked around comically, as though he were dancing to a tune he couldn't quite hear. All at once, his corpse collapsed to the ground, the undead now quite deceased.

Shanice stood in her place, Brad's head still in her hand, breathing hard and smiling. That had been fun, and it had relieved more tension than she realized she even had. Obviously, this guy had been causing her more grief than she knew, even though he brought her meals every night. That was a very small thing, in her life's grand scheme. Actually, it was the least he could do for all she had given him. The fact of the matter was that good help was simply too hard to find.

Almost in a trance-like state, she continued to stand there and feel the exhilaration of what she had just done, but after several minutes passed, she began to come back to reality. Taking a look around the yacht deck, Shanice quickly realized the mess she had made. Taking a deep breath, she flung Brad's head over the railing and into the ocean water, then set about doing the same with the body and cleaning up the disgusting slime that seemed to be everywhere.

As soon as she was finished cleaning, she looked down at herself and groaned. She was covered in filth, and it stunk like death, to top it all off. Here she worked, day in and day out to get rid of that smell on her own person. Now this idiot, who had betrayed her, managed to cover her in it without even trying. She would have to shower ten times just to get the smell off. She didn't even want to think about what she would have to do to make that go away.

Shanice propped the ruined mop against the railing and proceeded to take the water in the bucket and dumped it into the ocean water. In the bottom of the bucket remained about an inch of thick, black, bloody, sludgy body fluid that Brad had left behind. She would take care of that momentarily, dumping it as well. She had never been one to pay any mind to litter; as far as she was concerned, the planet belonged to her and she would do as she pleased. She didn't even give a second thought to whether or not the poisoned and dead blood would affect the sea life… she just didn't care. Besides, she needed to get the stink off of her right away; it was enough to gross out a zombie.

With the work done; she stripped off her now-ruined robe, mindlessly tossing it onto the deck while making her way to the shower. With Brad gone, she had quite a bit to do, so she needed to get cleaned up as soon as possible. She would have to get her own food, and now, thanks to him, she had to look for another minion. Building an army was turning out to be very slow and difficult work, but Shanice Hall was determined.

After all, she had revenge to exact, and time was steadily ticking.

CHAPTER 18

Life changed for the better for Mavis after coming clean with her parents. The biggest change of all was the release of all the heavy pressure she had constantly felt from sneaking around and lying all the time, from faking it. It had been horrible, though she hadn't realized just how horrible at the time. But once the cat was out of the bag, she knew she had been carrying a burden that was far too heavy for anyone to bear. She was glad it was done and over with.

Mavis' parents seemed much happier and more relieved as well. Everything about Mavis that had changed in the last year and a half could now be explained, from her strange taste in clothing to her odd appetite. They fell right into the swing of things and even teamed up with Matt to see to it that she had her food on time and regularly. The Harvey household indeed seemed to be getting back to normal, and it had been a long time coming.

But regardless of the newfound peace, Shanice was still out there. Police were looking for her as best as they could, having all-points-bulletins and warrants for her arrest, but it seemed that she had simply gone poof, and disappeared off the face of the earth once again. So, while the police continued to look, they also eased up, figuring that she had left the state and hopefully, given up on her threats of revenge. When they did find her, however, she would be locked up but good, and that was what Mavis was hoping for.

In the meantime, Mavis, Matt, and Kim continued their Kenpo training with Master Sheng. Kim was excelling far above and beyond what either of them or even Master Sheng, expected. The fact was that she was being eaten up inside by her grief over Shawn's death, and she was putting it to good use. For Kim, the quest against Shanice was more than just stopping a bad zombie; it was about taking her life as she had taken Shawn's. Though she hadn't voiced it, Mavis knew that Kim fully intended to be the one to end the girl once and for all.

∞

Kim was so detached… so different. Mavis' best friend was nothing like she used to be up until Shawn's murder. At one time, she had been the bouncy one who always wore a smile and always seemed to make others laugh at her own klutzy expense. At any given time she would be munching on chips, chocolate, or cookies, which provided her with her curvy figure. Kim had always worn her hair and makeup almost perfectly, and she carried a small, square mirror in her purse with which to check her look on a constant basis. Best of all, she wasn't the kind of girl who took life too seriously. It reflected poorly in her studies; but her dream was to one day marry, have babies, and stay at home raising mini-Kims. She would have been starting all of that in only weeks, if not for Shanice Hall and her attack on Kim's fiancé.

Now the girl was more often sullen than not. It showed in the fact that her curly hair was usually pulled back into a ponytail, and the only makeup she wore was a bit of mascara and lipstick, which never got checked and was gone by the end of the first period. She had gone from dresses to jeans and t-shirts, and there was no more laughter or tripping over her own feet. The good news was that Kim had been picking up her grades quite a bit, impressively so, in fact. Mavis attributed this to the fact that the work kept her mind off the reality.

To top it all off, she was dropping weight like mad, which Kenpo was accelerating, and she was becoming quite the martial artist in class with Master Sheng. Just a couple of weeks ago, she was trying to get the knack, and now she was given the most attention in class for her improving skills. She practiced alone, with Matt and Mavis, and with any other classmate who would let her try her hand at them.

Kim Coleman was a totally different person. It may not have been a good thing, but it wasn't all bad, either. When she looked at her friend, Mavis could see how life formed a person to be who they were.

Another change was that boys were looking at her much more often than ever before, even though Kim was extremely pretty. Mavis didn't know if it was her disposition or the way she carried herself, but Kim seemed to draw gazes at every turn. Unfortunately, no one in the tiny remaining senior class at Westside High had the courage to approach her, knowing what she had been through with Shawn Maher.

Another thing that was gone, maybe even the thing that Mavis loved the most, was Kim's smile and the dimples that formed when she flashed it. Now, she would simply turn up one side of her mouth when something humorous was said, or if she had to take pictures during an outing, or if someone was polite to her. But it was always obligatory and perfunctory, though no one would know it unless Kim Coleman was a person they knew well.

So, there was only one week until senior prom, and then a few more days until her class would graduate. Mavis thought of all the kids who would have been graduating this year, if not for their tragic deaths at their junior prom the year before. She wasn't sure if she could make it through the graduation ceremony. The knowledge alone was terribly hard to handle, and even though the passage of time seemed to dull the ache, it was something that she wasn't sure she could ever truly forgive herself for.

Prom was quickly approaching; at first, Kim hadn't intended to go, but she announced that week that she changed her mind. What if Shanice showed up to wreak havoc? Well, Kim wanted to be there, date or no date, so she too got herself a dress, and the three of them decided to go as a trio. Kim, Matt, and Mavis had worked diligently to formulate and agree on a plan, to drench each other in perfume, and to surround Mavis at all times. Mavis and Matt had their new clothes: matching goth style, of course. Even if Shanice didn't show up, it would be a lot of fun.

CHAPTER 19

It was Monday evening, just after supper. Mavis was in her room waiting for Kim, who was bringing over her prom dress. It was something of a tradition for the girls to get together and organize their looks, since before they even went to dances with dates. Back in those days, they simply went to the event together, whatever it was. Peas in a pod, they had been, but the last couple of years had managed to toss a lot of changes at both of them. They were both aware that their friendship was lacking something that neither of them could put their finger on.

A soft double-tap came on the bedroom door; Kim walked right in. She had her half-grin on her face, but tonight something was different: her eyes were alight! It was the first time in a long time that she had seen her friend's eyes glow, and rather than comment on them, she chose to enjoy the moment. Maybe it would be like old times for a short while.

"So! Where's the dress, girl?" Kim had hers in a protective sleeve over her arm. She gently laid it across Mavis' bed and then turned back to her. "You mean to tell me you don't even have yours ready to show?"

Sticking out her tongue, Mavis went to the closet and opened it. Reaching inside she drew out a covered dress as well and laid it next to Kim's. Both garments were sleeved in black, so the mystery was at its peak.

"Are you going to go first?" Kim asked. But without even waiting for an answer, she burst out, "Oh, geez. If you're not going to go, I'll go."

Immediately she began to unzip the cover; the girl was so excited she could hardly wait to get it out of the bag.

Mavis plopped down in the bean bag chair to hang out while Kim put on the dress. "So, are you feeling a little better about going?"

Kim shrugged her shoulders and kicked her jeans off her legs and feet, her smile gone. As she pulled her t-shirt over her head, she replied, "I don't know. Kind of hard to be really excited, all things considered. But I am psyched about the chance that Shanice might pop in and show her horrid face... so I can break it."

Mavis turned to Kim. "I have to tell you something. If she comes to the prom, you can't lay a hand on her. For one thing, you'd be arrested, and that's only if you survive. Kenpo or not, she's a zombie, Kim. She'll win."

Kim flashed her a look, but she didn't respond, and Mavis knew that the girl wasn't taking her words to heart. So, she dropped the subject, vowing to take it up with her another time. The last thing she wanted was to lose her best friend the way Shawn had been lost to them all.

The dress was form-fitting, red, and cut just above

the knee with a loose ruffled v-neckline. It had long sleeves, and of course, the obligatory but mild red glitter that set the dress off right. Once Kim had it on, she turned her back to Mavis to be zipped up.

"Do you want to go through my shoes?" Mavis asked as she zipped.

Kim whirled around and held her arms straight out. "Well? It's a size six, Mavis!"

She looked amazing, there were no two ways about it. "I didn't realize you had lost so much weight! Kim! You're always wearing those baggy clothes now, but you look incredible! You've lost a lot more weight than I realized. The Kenpo is really coming through for you."

"Thank you very much!" She put her hands on her hips and posed a bit here and there. "Mom and Dad let me go off the deep end. In my bag are shoes, a clasp bag, and matching jewelry. Here, I'll show you!"

Amused, Mavis adjusted herself in the beanbag chair, reclining slightly so she could get the full effect of the dress and accessories when Kim was done. It felt good to be doing this with her friend, and she decided then and there that she wouldn't ask Kim any more emotional questions about prom or Shawn; she would just be thankful for the fact that Kim was going, no matter what her personal motive was.

"So, I take it you're getting the full mani-pedi with hair and makeup," Mavis asked. "How are you going to do your hair?"

"Down," Kim replied as she clasped her necklace, which was a ruby heart surrounded by diamonds on a gold chain. It had a matching bracelet and earrings, too. "In all its curly, out of control glory, but I am going to use a couple of ruby clips on the sides that my mother got for Valentine's Day from dad a few years back. I brought them too."

Mavis listened to Kim ramble on about how she was having her hair done at the new place everyone was talking about on the outskirts of Greenville. It was a salon called "Up and Combing," and it was currently the talk of the female set at Westside. While Kim droned on about how she only wanted to be beautiful for Shawn's memory, or she would go in jeans and a t-shirt. Mavis listened and laughed responding to her friend in all the right places.

She looked magnificent, and both of the girls were impressed. Mavis admired Kim for several minutes before deciding to go show it to Jane.

CHAPTER 20

Shanice steered the small boat toward the yacht, which was still a good distance away. The radio blared, and behind her, the super-hot blond girl and Greek-god-looking guy were dancing and laughing as they sipped on wine coolers. She smiled to herself, amused at her next thought: what were their names again? Picking them up had only been decided on due to the guy's astronomical good looks, and the blond was a knockout herself. Shanice planned on turning him and taking him under her wing, and together the two of them would turn the blonde into supper and breakfast. Too bad, though; the girl would have made some guy very, very happy.

So, she was starting from scratch for the fourth time. First, there had been Candy's senseless demeanor, killed running out into the freeway after someone she thought to be Mavis Harvey. Next had been Gunnar, her first male minion and one she was convinced would be under her rule forever. Unfortunately, their attack on Mavis and her boyfriend resulted in his head getting caved in with a bat by Matt in a canine bite suit. Oh, well... so much for Gunnar.

Her third, of course, was Brad. Ah, she would miss his beautiful surfer-boy looks, but he wasn't very bright, and he was twice as defiant. Maybe in the real world, where people actually had heartbeats, men were the head of things overall. But in Shanice's new world, there was no one in charge but she, and she alone. The very idea that he thought he would ever again do as he pleased without asking her first made her want to laugh out loud, so she did. The couple behind her paused, looked at her, then rolled their eyes at each other. Shanice took no notice.

Naturally, thinking of Brad brought back the night of his ending. She sharply recalled the way it felt to tear his head from his body, and her stomach still roiled at the thought of the black goo all over her that had shot from his neck. He was dead, alright… rotten to the core inside, functioning only because of the daily nourishment she had forced him to bring. "Do I look like that inside?" she wondered to herself. Of course, she did; she was the same creature he was, the same as Mavis herself. They were all black inside… black and rancid.

Dragging her mind back to the present, Shanice realized they were almost to the yacht, close enough that it was time to focus fully on what she was doing. As she docked up next to it and tied the smaller vessel, she killed the motor and turned to her guests. Watching them for a moment, she realized they were enraptured with each other, and she felt a tinge of jealousy. It would be nice to fall in love, she thought, then she scoffed. She was no more capable of love than a housefly on spoils, and she knew it.

"Here we are, you two!" She stood there in her bikini, striking her sexiest pose to gain the man's attention. "Time to do some real partying. I've got all the party favors. Tonight is my treat; hopefully, I'll get treated in return."

The blond forgot about Mr. Wonderful and sensually walked over to Shanice. Lifting her right hand, she stroked Shanice's long dark curls and smiled. The girl only knew her by Miss Hall, but what did it matter. Who needed names, anyway? Shanice did.

"What's your name again, Cutie?" she asked the girl in a luring tone.

The hot blondie smiled and flicked her tongue rapidly over her lips with insinuation. "Melanna Goran," she replied in a hushed tone. "Behind me is Dalton Keene. You're Miss Hall, I never forget a name, especially when it's pinned to someone as luscious as you."

Oh, Shanice thought, this is going to be a lot of fun.

They all boarded the boat, speaking in flirtatious tones and cracking sexual jokes. Once on the deck, Shanice told them to make themselves completely at home, her casa was their casa. Dive into the food and drink. Want to wash off the saltwater? There were three showers. Mixed drinks and other alcoholic beverages could be found in the bar on the deck.

"I'll be back... I'm showering first."

While she scrubbed her body clean, she thought

about how she would bite Dalton and keep him for her own while Melanna showered. Once the girl came out of the shower, the three could begin to have a little fun together, but it was then that they would devour her.

The possibilities were endless. But one thing the two visitors agreed on when it came to the young Miss Hall, and the big yacht was having a little fun. The more they drank, the more focused they got on that part of the fun.

Before they knew it, Shanice was standing in the doorway, new robe on, hair damp, and an eye full of the activities they had been having for the last five minutes.

"Hi," Melanna greeted nervously when she looked up and saw Shanice. "That was fast; feel better?"

Shanice began to slowly walk toward them. "Of course. The salt on the skin is uncomfortable." She focused her gaze on Melanna, and with a deadly serious look in her eyes, she said, "I think it's your turn to freshen up, Mel."

The use of her nickname put her right at ease. "Sure thing. Just tell me where to go."

Shanice gave her the directions she needed, adding that she placed a sexy bikini and robe on the spare bed for her to wear. If she were cold, she would find warmer stuff in the dressers and closets. She should just act as though this were her "home away from home" and relax. She promised they were going to have a night that Melanna would never forget.

So, with a Cheshire cat grin on her smug, pretty face, the girl disappeared down into the living quarters to shower and basically dig through Shanice's things to her heart's delight. Shanice was neither naïve nor stupid; she knew that was what the girl would do, but she didn't mind. It would give her plenty of time to do what she would with Dalton. She turned to him with a smile on her face.

"So, Dalton… I guess it's just you and me, huh, Sexy?"

She always had been a quick thinker. She was alive, Brad was dead, and she was getting ready to begin her army again, starting with Dalton Keene.

∞

Kim grabbed her dress and bag before heading out to talk to Jane so that she could leave as soon as they were finished; it was getting late, and there was class tomorrow. Both had gotten so wrapped up in their prom dresses and the excitement they had felt at trying them on.

"So, we should try them on again tomorrow night?" Kim asked, holding the re-bagged dress out in gesture.

Mavis smiled. "Absolutely."

Jane was thrilled. She thought it was a brilliant plan, and she was blown away, she told the girls. "I have a volunteer project bright and early… oh, your breakfast is fresh and in the fridge. Sheep brains from that guy outside of town."

Mavis' mouth began to water, but she pushed the thought out of her mind.

"Thanks, Mom, yum, I'm not sure if I can wait till

morning, though." She turned to Kim. "So, see you at school in the morning, okay?"

With a nod, Kim gave her a light hug, considering her full arms, and then left. Mavis had a bit of raw chitterling, which she loved for the first time in her life, then she went to her room to turn in. As it turned out, she felt more tired than she had in a very long time.

She fell asleep thinking about Shanice and dreamed of the girl making a prom entrance straight into the arms of the cops.

CHAPTER 21

Shanice stirred in her bed on the yacht, then gave a leisurely stretch and satisfied moan. She typically didn't sleep like that, long, deep, and dreamless, but she did for once. Attributing it to all the alcohol she drank the night before with Dalton and Melanna, she swung her feet to the floor and headed directly for the shower. One thing about being a zombie: one got smelly very easily. After all, she was in the perpetual process of rotting. It made her sick just to think about it. She had been the most beautiful girl at Greenville High. She was still very attractive, thanks to makeup, her looks were fading, and it was hard to cover up.

She stepped into the hot water and moaned as she carefully washed her dead, flaking skin with a soft washcloth. She thought about last night; it hadn't quite turned out as she had planned. As soon as Melanna went to shower, she had torn into the back of Dalton's neck with her teeth while under the guise of giving him a massage. His change started fast... almost right away, and it was startling. While she raced to explain to him what she had done, Melanna had been hiding around the corner, listening. Who knew how long she had been watching? She had stepped out with confidence, expressed her deep, heartfelt admiration for what was happening, and proceeded to beg Shanice for the change. She gladly bestowed it upon the girl. After all, a true army consisted of more than two people. The only setback was the fact that Melanna was going to be their meal; now they had to go hunt. With plenty of alcohol on board, they took the small boat and kidnapped a guy walking to his hut on the beach by way of an isolated trail. Together they ate, went back to the yacht, and partied until dawn.

Shanice had been sure to lecture them during that time about being the queen bee. She made sure they understood that she would rip their heads off if they got out of line, and she wouldn't hesitate. They should never consider crossing her, and their job was to do her bidding. That was as far as it went, though; she would fill them in on her situation with Mavis Harvey and their role in it another time when they were better at living their new "lives."

When she got out of the shower, Shanice grabbed her fluffiest robe and wrapped it around her constantly ice-cold body. Suddenly, she could hear the voices of Melanna and Dalton. They were talking about something that was unintelligible to her, but she could hear them laughing every now and then. Shanice wondered what they were up to. Well, time to get dressed and go find out. She figured a bikini would do fine for now; besides, all she planned to do was grab some of the leftovers they brought back last night after the kill. Then she would let the sun warm her until it was time to run her errands. Today was the one day of the week she took the boat to Kingston and checked her post office box.

Within fifteen minutes, Shanice stepped onto the deck and into the bright sunlight. It was afternoon, so she wasn't surprised that it was already so beautiful outside. She made her way to her lounger and plopped down casually. Immediately, she was greeted by Melanna.

"You slept hard," she greeted. "I looked in on you several times to make sure you were alright. I hope it's okay that Dalton and I ate; we saved you the very best leftovers of the lot, though. Are you hungry?"

"Ravenous."

Melanna smiled and nodded, then disappeared from the deck as she made her way to the galley. In minutes she was back, carrying a tray with a covered plate, a mimosa, and plenty of wet napkins. Setting the tray over Shanice's lap, she waited for her to take the cover off and approve. Shanice did so, and there on the tray was the freshest looking pile of brain matter she had ever seen. It looked absolutely wonderful.

"Amazing," Shanice said. "This will do just fine, thank you."

The girl smiled again. "Dalton is working out down under with the weights. If you don't need me for anything, I'm going to join him."

Impressed with her level of submission, Shanice replied, "This is perfect. After I eat I am going to be taking the boat to Kingston; I have some errands to run and will be gone for a while. Do as you like, but make sure you don't move the yacht an inch… understood?"

"Of course."

With that, Melanna disappeared, and Shanice took the next twenty-minutes to consume the brains. Soon, she felt like a million dollars, and her plate was completely clean. Putting the tray aside, she went to get dressed so she could head to Kingston. Her small box was probably overflowing, and there were certainly bills to be paid. As pleased as she was thus far with Dalton and Melanna and the loyalty they had shown in only one night, she knew she was on the right track with her "army." It just wouldn't do to draw negative attention to herself by blowing off her worldly responsibilities.

Heading to her sleeping quarters, Shanice set about getting dressed so she could make her way inland to the post office. She was also expecting an update phone call from Sonny Maneli at any time, and could hardly wait to hear what he had to say regarding the hopeful "outing" of Mavis by the emergency room doctors. Certainly, her parents would have her locked up or studied, or something, thereby doing half the work for Shanice before she even figured out her next step.

As long as they left the girl herself for Shanice to have her way with, she really didn't care.

∞

Shanice sat in her car, and with a smile on her face and a whistle on her lips, she jumped from the rental car she kept for in-town travels. She locked the door behind her, and walked into the post office and went to the first open window. There, she requested that all mail to her box be held, the box is suspended, and that the workers there wait for her to put in a change of address for her new box. She strolled out of the office, still smiling and whistling. After that, Shanice parked her rental at the dock and got back onto her boat. It was time to find a nice, new beach to rest on, one that was far away from Kingston, Jamaica.

∞

The next three days seemed to drag by slowly as they waited. Kim, Matt, and Mavis went on with their schedules, going to school, Kenpo, and practicing together, all while waiting on the edge of their seats constantly for graduation day. They didn't speak of it or ponder the possibilities, for fear it might jinx the whole thing, but they silently wondered to themselves. The most interesting thing they did was finally get to show each other's prom clothes off, and even Matt joined in this time around.

It was Wednesday, late in the evening, when the three of them all met in Mavis' bedroom with their outfits. Playing dress up for the third time that week, you could tell they were all on pins and needles. As suspected, both Mavis and Matt went the goth-type route: Mavis' dress consisted of a tight leather bodice with long flowing lace skirt and sleeves. She topped it off with black granny boots, dangling black chain earrings, and a simple velvet choker. Matt went with an all-black tux but opted for a single ruby stud in his left ear.

As for Kim, she still looked great in her red dress, and even better when she added all of her accessories. Though they were having a blast, by eleven-thirty they were forced to break up the party since they had school the following day. Matt drove Kim home, and they all parted ways.

But Mavis didn't sleep well. She was tense, and she knew it, and it was all centered around the fact that Shanice Hall may or may not come to the prom. Mavis wanted her to, but she really didn't want her to at the same time. Truthfully, she just wanted Shanice to disappear, just forget about her anger and need for revenge. Maybe she would just try to live some kind of life as a zombie like Mavis was doing. In her heart, she knew that Shanice wouldn't stop until one of them was likely dead.

In her dreams that night, Shanice did appear at the prom. She dreamed it over and over again, each time with a different, equally disturbing climax. She pulled herself violently from each one, feeling emotional and shaken every time. It was a good thing her body didn't depend on sleep to survive because she slept horribly that night.

Thursday morning, she got up and got ready to face the world, like she did every other day, but on this morning, fragments of nightmares flashed continually through her mind. She had to force a smile when she went out to breakfast and even had to force it when her mother gave her raw kidney and lung from some poor beast. It was delicious, but it gave her no pleasure whatsoever.

Matt showed up in his old car at the usual time, and together they hopped into Mavis' convertible, with Matt in the driver's seat. A quick jolt and they arrived at Kim's, and with her in the car, the three of them arrived at school ten minutes later. Except for greetings, the entire ride was quiet, the radio playing softly in the background. Obviously, it wasn't just Mavis; the other two were just as tense, and the tension grew as prom night drew nearer.

The day dragged on, but it always did right at the end of the school year. The energy was high in everyone, and it was hard for students to contain themselves as they should. High school was almost over; college was just around the bend. But for Mavis, she remained still all day, and finally resigned herself to being powerless in the situation. Shanice Hall and Mavis were going to have their day, whether it was this Saturday at prom or some other time; it would happen. But living day to day with the shadow of Shanice's threat hanging over her was too much for her to bear. By the fifth period, she made a firm decision to let it go, so she put the entire thing out of her mind and turned her focus to all of the wonderful, once-in-a-lifetime things that were happening in her life.

Finally, she was invigorated, cheerful, and felt burden-free. Any thoughts of Shanice were gone from her mind completely. It was time to laugh and smile.

Mavis had enough of the pits.

Turning to a mousy brown haired girl, Karen Barnes, she smiled and asked, "So, are you looking forward to prom this year, or what?"

∞

"Mom, I'm home!"

Mavis flung her bag to the floor next to the umbrella stand and used the heel of her combat boot to gently kick the front door shut. Behind her, Matt's car was getting more distant, and Mavis smiled to herself as she thought of the kisses he had just given her.

"Mom?"

The house sounded completely empty, so she turned her attention to the small wall nook which served as a place to leave notes and mail for those who were to arrive. As she expected, a note from her mother sat loosely atop an average-sized pile of envelopes.

"Dear Mavis Luv,

I'm working with the women's shelter doing data entry, so I'll be just a bit late.

Love you,
Mommy"

Mavis smiled and rolled her eyes at her mother's use of the term "mommy." Of course, Mavis had stopped regularly using it years ago, but Jane often joked how she missed those years. Every note she wrote was signed in this way, and it always cheered Mavis' heart to see it, no matter how goofy it was.

She gave a final chuckle and headed to the kitchen to see what Mom left for her. As she went, she dialed Matt's number. He might not be home yet, and he wouldn't answer if he were driving. But on the third ring, he did pick up, to her surprise.

"Hey, beautiful," he greeted.

If she could have blushed, she would have. They chatted on for a couple of minutes.

CHAPTER 22

Montego Bay sounded like the perfect choice to her, so she, Dalton, and Melanna secured the ship and took the yacht to that very place. She didn't want anything to do with being around the other vessels, who stayed close together for the sake of partying. Instead, she made sure she was on the fringes, yet still a bit in sight so as to not look suspicious.

Once that was done, Shanice boated to shore and got a rental car, a little blue sedan that was attractive but common and low-key. It was that vehicle which she drove to the nearest post office and rented a post office box, this time for only thirty days. She had no idea what would happen in the future; there was no sense in getting too overzealous. Shanice appeared focused and motivated as she took care of one business issue after another, like a robot.

Every time the thought of senior prom came up she pushed it away, but it was persistent, and she was prideful. How satisfying would it be to look Mavis in the eyes, in front of the remaining class that the girl didn't shred apart, and basically instill dread in her, but keep her guessing. The thought became more and more tantalizing with each passing second.

After renting the box and putting in a change of address form for her aliases, she hit the grocery store. The only thing she bought there was a variety of wines and liquors, which she loaded into the trunk of the sedan in boxes. Supper wasn't a concern; her new soldiers were privy to what their task was when it came to feeding, so they did the work and she came first.

Continually, as she went, she thought about the prom… not primarily, but the thought was hiding in the dark corners of her mind, and it was tugging away. She visualized Mavis trembling before her, knowing that her friends and family were all gone. Then, she would pounce, and end Mavis' life (or death, as it were) for good. With Mavis gone and her army behind her, the world would be Shanice's playground.

Shanice transferred her goods to the boat, then took her car the half-block jaunt to the garage, where she safely parked and locked it. Hopping into the boat, she set off for the yacht, which was waiting about fifteen minutes from shore. The sun was just beginning to go down, and occupants of the boats around her were beginning to cut loose and have fun. She was in the mood to do the same. Speeding up, she wondered what condition the yacht would be in, considering her minions were practically brand new. Oh, well, it would be a good test. Hopefully, they turned out to be as diligent as they were this morning when she woke.

As she got nearer and nearer to the yacht and prepared to dock, she no sooner finished tying off than she looked up and saw the smiling and paling faces of her two new sidekicks, Melanna and Dalton. They were smiling down at her, but only for a fraction of a second before Dalton started down the ladder to assist her.

"Go ahead and go up," he said in a cheerful voice. "I'll unload the supplies. I hope all went simply and easily for you in Montego today."

She was going to have to talk to them about more than just the zombie situation; she wanted to come clean with them about the whole truth. After all, she needed to be able to trust them. If the truth is known, she already did; they both seemed thoroughly devoted to her. Shanice already believed she could trust them with the reality of not only her true identity, but the situation with her parents, and her future plans for her mortal enemy, whom she had also left out of the story thus far.

But as she stepped onto the deck, she thought she would wait until later that evening. For now, there were supplies to be attended to, and she was going to fill them in on some new and surprising plans she had just firmly decided on, as well as the responsibilities they would have while she carried out those plans. Shanice was sure they would be as excited as she was. There was nothing like a bit of drama-filled intimidation to make one's day complete.

Before getting to all of that, she took a good look around the spotless deck, which was so clean that the deck light seemed to glisten off its surface. While Dalton busied himself with unloading the supplies from the boat, Melanna assisted by putting things away in their proper places. Shanice, on the other hand, went below deck to check out the living quarters and see if they were left in any kind of disarray. Much to her pleasant surprise, the entire vessel was immaculate, from front to back and in every crevice and corner.

When Shanice arrived back on deck, both Dalton and Melanna stood waiting at attention, their hands clasped behind their backs. Both of them were silent, their eyes fixed on her unflinchingly as they waited for her to either tell them what to do next or simply speak the first word. She smiled to herself as she realized that, for the first time since this craziness began, she had finally found herself a couple of real soldiers. Yes, she was definitely on the right track this time, and she loved it.

"Relax, you two!" She walked up to both of them and touched each of them on their arms gently. "At least for a little bit. You've done an outstanding job on the boat; I'm blown away. You deserve to relax and have a drinkie or two before you head inland to find dinner."

"We have dinner ready and waiting."

Shanice stopped cold, and her smile faded, but more out of surprise than anything else. She looked at them both incredulously, waiting for one of them to start giggling, like the statement had been a joke, but they both maintained their stoic expressions.

"What do you mean, dinner is ready and waiting?" she asked. "Do you mean you hunted while I was inland? Before the sun went down?"

Melanna turned and looked at her without changing her expression. "A man was swimming alone in the alcove around the bend. Dalton was swimming as well, while I was cleaning. When he returned, he had the man with him, so we took him under and tied him up in the dry storage. He'll be good and fresh by the time we are ready to eat."

At first, all she could do was look at them in disbelief and surprise. Then, slowly, she began to smile. This was simply too good to be true! Yes, they had earned the surprise she had for them, though it would also serve as something of a test of their true loyalty and obedience. But she had left them alone on the yacht without knowing what to expect at all, and what she found when she returned was nothing short of miraculous.

They were up to the challenge already, after only a couple of days.

"Wonderful," she replied, beaming. "Then I say we have some cocktails and relax for a while; he'll keep." All three of them burst out laughing at her bad joke. "In the meantime, Melanna, why don't you make us all a drink; you know what we like. Then we can all sit down together so I can fill you in on my day, which has been very interesting indeed. I have something to tell you... something I think will please you both very much. So, we'll chat a bit before we devour Swimmer Boy down there."

Another round of laughter erupted as Melanna went

to the bar for the drinks. Shanice took her lounger, and Dalton got comfortable in a deck chair which was paired with another, both situated across from Shanice. It made her feel like a queen to have them submit to her this way. She was very relaxed, happy, and pleased with the two of them. They were both gorgeous to look at, and Dalton's physique made him a bit imposing; they would be the perfect ones to accompany her on a short in and out jaunt to Greenville, on Saturday night.

But for now, she would fill them in on her day, her thoughts, and her weekend plans.

CHAPTER 23

Thursday flew by and surprisingly enough, the two had braced themselves for Kim to be upset. Mavis and Matt were worried about Kim, and her mourning the death of Shawn somehow coming back so close to prom. Her responses had been stiff, but overall, she had been calm, cool, and collected. Only Mavis truly understood that she was much more upset than she was demonstrating. This was the new Kim, the calmer, more disciplined, and contemplative Kim.

The worst part was that Mavis feared that Kim would break down at the last minute. Kim reassured her that she was now looking forward to the dance for its own sake. On some level, she admitted, she felt like it was time to try to have some fun and get on with her life. Nothing was going to change by her checking out of dating and socializing.

With that particular cloud gone from over their heads, the three of them began to get a bit giddy about Saturday night. It was exciting, after all: their senior prom! They had made solid plans to ride together in Mavis' convertible, and that both Mavis and Kim would spend their Saturday morning getting their hair and nails done. Matt would be working at the pack that morning, and besides, he insisted he had everything under control in the prom department, and he could do his own hair.

∞

Shanice suddenly heard a sound…

A boat motor, coming from the distance. Naked, she peeked around the corner of the cabin door and saw a boat with four people coming at her at a high rate of speed. They were yelling and waving their arms, but she wasn't really concerned, it was dinner.

Yes, dinner has arrived.

She grabbed up her robe and put it on, giggling as she did so. Next, she grabbed her drink; soon, she was in character, and the boat drew near and sidled alongside. She looked down with a smile covering her face. "Hello!"

Shanice Hall would handle them like a pro.

She just knew it.

Anyway, the yacht would be a crime scene for a bit. Not to worry, Shanice, she told herself. Her new minions Melanna and Dalton would take care of the mess. They would be fine, no matter what, and everything would turn out to be exceptional; she could guarantee it.

∞

Before any of them knew it, it was Friday morning, the day before the much-awaited senior prom.

Mavis was simply beside herself. Here it was, finally.

Truth be told, she didn't think she'd ever make it to this point in her educational career, but she assumed that most everyone felt that way. But here it was, and she was relishing the fact.

For the first time in months, Mavis thought that things might be going the way she had always wanted them to go. She wanted normal, but being a zombie made that goal a bit difficult to achieve. But finally, after all the chaos and confusion about what and who she was, she was getting ready for the senior prom, and Mavis couldn't have been more satisfied. The thought of Shanice showing up to the dance had been a dreadful one indeed; now she didn't even worry about that.

Today was the last day of school! After that, they had the prom, and then graduation ceremonies that coming week. Seniors who passed and would graduate wouldn't attend Monday through Friday, like the freshman, sophomore, and junior classes were. As of the end of the class day today, they would be free of their "lower" educations at last!

But Mavis also had another, darker thought. She wondered what the prom would look and feel like with most of the kids who should be in attendance dead, dead at her own hand at junior prom the year prior. There was still a handful of students who survived the ordeal by not attending at all, then, of course, there was Mavis and Kim. Several new students had also enrolled, with great trepidation from the stories, but to everyone's surprise, the senior class indeed added several to their numbers. At one time, there were over two-hundred-thirty students in the Greenville High School's Class, but now she would be surprised if there were one-hundred. The thought of it all made her heartache and her stomach queasy, and it was all she could do to push the thoughts out of her head. The last thing she wanted was to slide backward emotionally and mentally, thinking negative thoughts about things that she was powerless to change.

No, she had far too much going well for her now, even with Shanice's threats and looming existence. Even if she had to do it over and over again, she would take control of her fear, apprehension, and resentment when it came to Shanice Hall. She would live for the moment and the day, and she would deal with that girl when, and if, she ever decided to make good on her threats.

That Friday morning, Mavis sat at the kitchen table with her mother, eating a small portion of raw cow tongue and a piece of beef kidney. Her mom never complained about the disgusting fare that her daughter's body required; she simply averted her eyes and looked through the sliding glass doors to the backyard. Mavis knew she was repulsed. The woman had given her a look that told her that she was just as relieved to have her in their lives.

While Jane and Todd realized that the day would come, that the two girls would have another confrontation, and it scared them to death that there was nothing they could do about it. Like Mavis, they had to roll with the punches.

On this morning, the last day of Mavis' high school

career, Jane chatted with her daughter about that topic, as well as the upcoming prom. It was a beautiful spring morning, and Mavis felt good about all that the day stood for. She was in a wonderful mood, and anxious for Matt to arrive so they could pick up Kim and get on with their day. After all, that was the only way they were going to put the darn thing behind them.

"Is Kim the cutest ever in her prom dress, or what?" Jane was now starting to make more eye contact with her daughter since the girl had just taken her licked-clean plate to the sink, where she rinsed it and put it in the dishwasher.

Standing at the counter, she drained the rest of her milk before answering her mother's question. "I know it! It's almost unbelievable, the weight she's lost; she looks amazing!" Mavis rinsed her milk glass and put it in the dishwasher as well.

"Adorable," Jane mumbled as she shook her head. "Just adorable. But she certainly is a lot more... aloof... then she used to be, isn't she Mav?"

Mavis wiped her mouth and checked her face in the marbled mirror hanging over the back of the sink in fancy squares. "Yeah, she is. Aloof is a good word, too. I think it's just going to take her a little more time, and we know she'll never forget Shawn or what happened to him. But one thing is for sure: she is starting to come out of her bubble a tiny little bit, aloof or not."

Jane hopped up for another cup of coffee. "How can you tell?"

Mavis leaned back against the counter with a smile on her face. "Well, when Matt and I were getting ready to tell her about us going to the prom, we had braced ourselves for her to be very upset. Come to find out, she wanted to go also, but the main reason she wanted to go was that she thought there was a chance the evil girl would show up anyway." Mavis paused there for effect, her smile intact. Jane was giving her an impatient look after a moment, so she continued. "Not only that, she said she wanted to still go to prom, and not for the sake of Shanice, but for the sake of the dance itself."

Jane breathed a sigh of relief. "It does sound like things are going in the right direction with her grief. But I don't think a day will ever come that Shanice would be able to be in the same room as Kim Coleman and not run the risk of getting her butt kicked, at least."

Mavis chuckled. "I'd have to agree."

Right then, the doorbell from the front door chimed loudly... Matt was there. Mavis gave her mother a hug and kiss, thanked her for breakfast, then jogged to the front door to head off to school. It was strange not toting a bag with her, but there would be free time in all classes today. Mavis thought there might be treats, not that it mattered to her, but treats always made things seem more festive and party-like. In all honesty, she was always likely to eat the snacks at school functions just to satisfy the urge to eat, in essence fooling her own mind.

The entire day would consist of fond farewells and boys wrestling between the desks to let out their energy. Her bag wasn't needed, but a kiss from Matt was, and she planted one on him as soon as she opened the door.

"Are you ready to get this over with?" he asked as soon as they broke their kiss.

"Like nothing else," Mavis replied.

As an afterthought, Mavis turned and waved goodbye to her mother. "See ya later, Mom!"

Jane waved back, coffee at her lips, limiting her words of response. She wouldn't have had time anyway; the kids were out the door and safe on the other side of it before she even knew they were gone. She smiled at the closed door and thought about her beautiful daughter, soon to be a grown woman. The very thought of Mavis eventually moving away from her and Todd nearly made her shake with fear. Jane had lived a very abundant, safe, and peaceful life, but she knew the truth of the world. The truth that out there, outside of that heavy oak suburban front door, monsters were running around all over the place and only a couple of them that she knew of were zombies. So, she worried about her daughter's welfare and future as any parent did.

With a sigh, Jane made her way back out to the kitchen with her coffee cup. Not only were her daughter's hands full these days, but so were hers, as always. She stopped at the calendar hanging on the wall by the fridge and took note that she had a volunteer obligation at the homeless shelter at 10:30; she had signed on to help serve the noon meal.

Jane also hoped, briefly, that she had instilled enough character into Mavis for her to know how important it was to keep busy and be productive;

sometimes it was the only thing that kept a person from falling apart.

CHAPTER 24

Just as Mavis and her two sidekicks suspected, the school was abuzz with energy and impatience from the first second the students began to pass through the large double doors. Everyone in the senior class was ready to put good old Westside behind them, and though they had survived thirteen years of formal education, they acted as though the next seven hours would never pass. Their enthusiasm for the occasion was highly contagious, resulting in the juniors, sophomores, and freshmen being just as loud and obnoxious as they.

It was an invigorating rush, to say the least. From the very first bell, everything seemed surreal to Mavis. There was absolutely no studying or silence of any kind. Kids were free to talk, ramble around their classrooms, and play games. As Mavis had suspected, there were plenty of homemade and store-bought treats to snack on in each class. By the third period, she was completely bloated, though not satisfied.

Even though everyone else was gorging themselves as well, each student's lunch was completely scarfed down. As soon as the lunch rotation was complete, all of the students were steered outside, one class at a time in a very disorderly fashion, to the football field. There, the faculty of Westside, along with student volunteers, had set up a small-scale carnival, with several games and crazy competitions to help the students pass the rest of the day without killing the teachers.

Just when it didn't seem possible that it would ever happen, and all of the kids had, at last, pushed all hope of being released from their hostage situation from their minds, the principal took to a wood box with a microphone and silenced the crowd. When he had the voices down to a dull roar, he delivered a short, but effective speech to all of the students, making special mention of the seniors who "had endured so much" during their years at their beloved Westside High. When he was finally finished, the last bell rang shrilly throughout the campus, and all of the students, Mavis and her friends included, ran for the building, their belongings, and their freedom.

∞

Mavis, Matt, and Kim went bursting through the double doors, out into the bright sunlight, their arms in the air and screams flying from their lips. They were surrounded by countless others doing the same, and while the din was deafening to the adults, they were all smiling as they held their hands over their ears. The students were oblivious to the adults' presence; they were released!

By the time the three of them reached the car, they were out of breath, wanting to laugh but unable to because they couldn't inhale properly. Matt sat down hard on the rear bumper, while both girls leaned against the vehicle until they could catch their breath. After that, they roared with laughter at the wonder and excitement of it all. It had been such a plain, empty, unproductive day, but it had been one of the most fulfilling of Mavis' life.

"Now the prom," she said when the laughter died, and her voice sounded almost sad.

The other two got quiet immediately. As the parking lot quickly cleared out, leaving only the three of them and a few stragglers either walking or biking, the only sound that could be heard was their ragged breathing. But the silence said a lot… it said that prom was the final thing that settled it. Yes, this part of their lives was almost over and behind them for good, and they had a boundless future ahead of them to look forward to. But it was sad, even bittersweet, nonetheless.

"Yeah," Kim agreed. "Prom."

The sadness and loneliness that Kim felt inside could be heard in her tone. Mavis scooted over to be nearer to her, then put her arm over Kim's shoulder and gave her a half-hug. Leaning her head on Kim's shoulder, she remained still just long enough to let it sink in that she was near and there for her.

"This is gonna sound really dumb," Mavis finally said in a low voice, "and I know it isn't going to succeed in doing anything but sounding ancient and cliché, and I'm sorry ahead of time for that. But Kim, there will be someone else for you… I just know it."

Kim stared at her feet. "I know it, too. But it doesn't make all this any easier."

They sat in silence for a short time longer, then they finally piled in the car. It was Friday, and their Kenpo class had been canceled due to school letting out for the seniors. Master Sheng had a senior of his own who attended Westside, and his family had special plans for the student. Once they were off and down the road, they decided that they would practice Kenpo together for one hour, then they would get something to eat, maybe Sports Burger.

With the top down, the three headed for Mavis' house, taking the long way to get there. They had the music playing and the wind whipped through their hair as all three sang along to the song pumping from the speakers. Today was a day to celebrate and be happy, and tomorrow's prom celebration was a reason as well.

So, they drove on, ignoring the pain for the pleasure.

CHAPTER 25

While Matt was steering Mavis' car away from the school with the top down, Shanice Hall and her two obedient soldiers were picking up a rental car from the Toledo Rental Ride at the airport. They had just come in from Jamaica, landing while Westside's students were having a blast at the mini carnival. With them was an abundance of luggage, though they didn't intend to stay past Sunday, at which time they would catch a flight back out. They would only toy with Mavis and her friends on prom night; after that, they would get back to the yacht until such a time as Shanice thought it was proper to advance in her "war."

As expected, she had heard from Sonny Maneli, who was only able to tell her that Mavis and her friends appeared to be completely focused on their upcoming prom dance. He had nothing new for her that she couldn't get herself, so she dismissed him for the time being, telling him to wait for her call.

Melanna and Dalton stood a good ten feet behind her at the Rental Ride counter, waiting for her to sign her name to the paperwork. Fortunately for Shanice, they were just as excited about the facts of their current situation as she was, maybe more, since she had filled them in on the details of their mission. After all, imagine partying in Jamaica, trying to live it up before the world went up in a ball of fire from World War Three, then joining a pretty woman on her yacht and becoming an immortal zombie. Sure, there were setbacks... like the incessant hunger. But overall, they both felt magnificent, strong, as if they could take over the world, and that was just what Shanice promised they would do... once they eliminated this Mavis girl. They couldn't do it on their own, however. Neither of them consisted of much more than exquisite good looks and the basic understanding of language; they just weren't that bright or that gutsy. But this Shanice had all of that in spades, and they were more than willing to follow her all the way to the top. As far as Shanice was concerned, they were chumps, and everyone she ever turned would be a chump. But these two knew how to respect her authority, so they would certainly do for now.

After about twenty-minutes, Shanice approached them with a handful of contract paperwork on the rental car and a set of keys in her hand. The smile on her face told her it was all a go, so as she walked past them, pretending they didn't exist, they simply grabbed the luggage and followed her out through a side door and into a parking lot full of rentals.

The pair followed her to a specific lane of cars that looked as though they had been, at least, gently used. It didn't take long to reach a beige sedan that appeared to be a couple of years old. Dalton turned to Melanna, and they both made a face at each other; Melanna, who was the most talkative of the pair, was the first to speak.

"Um, Shanice… this is the car?"

Shanice paused and turned to look at Melanna, a stern expression on her face that was filled with disgust.

"Do you trust me, or not?" she asked, a slight sneer in her voice.

Dalton was the one to answer. "Of course, we do, Shanice. It's just that… well, wouldn't this type of car attract the wrong kind of attention?"

Shanice pressed the button on the key fob that unlocked the door, then turned to them both and smiled. "Always remember: when it comes to our mission, I am way ahead of you. I know and understand things about the situation and location we are at that you have no idea about. Now, a newer car is what they will be looking for when they are trying to track me down, so it's best to simply rent something a bit older and look less conspicuous."

Her sidekicks nodded dumbly and waited for her to pop the trunk so they could load the luggage.

As they climbed into the car, Shanice continued. "We will be staying at a hotel called the 'Reasonable Inn'; I will have my own room, you two will share. They are adjoining rooms. It, like the car, is not a top of the line place of accommodation, though they do have an outdoor pool. The law, or anyone else trying to locate me, will look at the fancier places, so this is it…

"Also, I don't expect that the law will be putting much effort into tracking me down. We really have nothing to worry about, but I like playing it safe."

Soon, Shanice was pulling out of the lot and heading for the hotel, which turned out to be only four blocks from the airport. They checked into their rooms, unpacked, and then had a short meeting in Shanice's quarters.

"Well, we have a free evening before the big confrontation," she began. "I say we each have a couple of cocktails, then you two can head out and get supper. I suggest using the river for dumping when the time comes. I would do your hunting down at the Roller Tavern, by the dam. You'll find an easy target or two. It will be convenient to dispose of them since that particular bar is only three blocks from here… got it?"

With vigorous nodding, the two agreed with her, then Melanna got up to make the drinks she suggested. "We'll need showers before we go find dinner," she said.

"Of course."

Within an hour, the two of them left, and Shanice started on her second cocktail while she opened the zipper bags containing their formal wear for the prom, which she had picked up in Montego Bay right before catching their flight. Dalton and Melanna would match, both wearing navy and gray. She even bought them matching corsages. Her dress was green, however, about as green as it could get. Her corsage was a white carnation. Tacky, but she loved the smell, and it took a bit of the harshness away from the dress. After laying out the clothing and all accessories, she looked it all over and smiled. She would certainly look like she belonged; she and her pals would wait in the parking lot for that little Mavis.

Yes, indeed. Before it was all said and done, Mavis and her friends would pay for her losses. They would pay for the fact that she was the undead now. They would pay for the death of Gunnar. But most of all, they would pay for taking Candace from her and making her seek out new friends for all eternity.

Shanice Hall could hardly wait for prom. Of course, she wouldn't have a date, but she had no interest in one, especially since she wouldn't be able to get in and didn't like to dance. She wouldn't be missing out on the food, because it would all be either cooked or pre-prepped… yuck! She also couldn't care less about running into old pals or associates… that would be the last thing she needed since the entire area was on the lookout for her to have her arrested. It was that fact alone that motivated her to purchase bleach for her hair before leaving Jamaica. Right now, while her two underlings were out getting their supper, that she would change her hair color. This would make her much less identifiable, considering she was a deep brunette naturally.

Shanice spent the next couple of hours playing dress up and drinking all by herself. It really wasn't the fact that she drank that stood out, it was the fact that, before she became a zombie, she could get drunk quite easily. Now it seemed that she couldn't at all, and it was frustrating to her, and she found herself drinking from sunup until sundown just for show. Must have something to do with being dead, she thought to herself.

After making yet another drink, she took the clothing she had chosen for Melanna and Dalton and put the items in their room on their bed, then went back to her own area and turned the radio on the alarm clock up loud. Next, she began to try on her own outfit. Though she had done it once, right before they left on the plane, she wanted to play dress up again, so she danced around the room and dolled herself up in her prom clothing. When she was finished, she thought about what a shame it was that she wouldn't actually be attending the dance; the boys would love her. She was the most gorgeous girl on the planet.

Before she knew it, Dalton and Melanna returned to the room with a woman in her early twenties. While Shanice didn't prefer female meat, and neither did Melanna, it was a bit too risky to bring and kill two people in a hotel room. The best bet was to settle for what they got, and it appeared that this was it. Young women were much easier to lure under the guise of a good party than men were, especially when there was a hot guy like Dalton doing the luring.

So, for the next hour, the three of them entertained the young woman with alcohol, music, and bad jokes. She easily began to get drunk and sloppy, which made Shanice frustrated and motivated her to end the whole charade quickly. The first opportunity they got was when she excused herself to stagger to the bathroom. The three of them were on her like vultures on a cadaver. It happened so quickly that the girl didn't even have time, nor the presence of mind, to utter a peep.

They knocked her unconscious, then took her into the bathroom in Dalton and Melanna's room. They would devour her in the bathtub; it simply wouldn't do to mess up the carpeting in one of the main rooms. The bathroom would be much easier to clean, and so they could eat without worry or stress. Shanice demanded that they save her kidneys and liver for the morning, which they saved in zipper baggies in the small refrigerator in her room, then they were finally able to dig in.

By the time they were finished and had eaten their fill, the bathroom looked like the crime scene that it was. Shanice casually strolled out of their side of the room into her own, ordering them to get the bathroom cleaned up. Dalton pointed out that they had no cleaning supplies, and needed to dump the body, so she sent him, with money, to purchase the needed items; Melanna went along to make sure he got everything they needed. The pair cleaned up just enough to get away with a trip out in public, then left. While they were gone, Shanice took a long, hot shower and then relaxed with another drink.

By the time she finished that beverage and made a new one, Dalton and Melanna could be heard in their room, likely doing the cleaning she had directed them to complete. She listened to them chatter, then finished it and made a third. Finally, she got tired of the sound of their muffled voices and turned the clock radio back on, letting the music drown them out. Letting her mind turn back to the prom, she glanced at the time and decided it was almost time to try and get a little rest; she wanted to be at her prime when she faced that little vixen Mavis.

Shanice Hall fell asleep with her drink in her hand, spilling it all over her bedspread. She didn't sleep well, however. Her slumber was filled with dreams of eventual defeat and permanent death, and more than once she woke with worry on her mind.

CHAPTER 26

Beginning Friday evening, Mavis found herself really beginning to loosen up, both mentally and emotionally, about prom. By the time she went to bed and began to doze off, the thought of Shanice Hall either showing up or not showing up started to become a distant and unimportant thought. Finally, by Saturday morning, her enemy was the furthest thing from her mind. It was beginning to look like Kim was letting go of her hang-ups about the situation as well. Matt was just happy-go-lucky and chipper; he couldn't have been more eager or happy if he tried.

As they had planned, the three of them practiced Kenpo on Friday while listening to heavy metal. Kim was really starting to pull away from the songs with more "poppy" sounds, and she was leaning more and more toward what Mavis referred to as 'angry music' every day. It seemed to fit her new disposition, and believe it or not, she seemed to thrive on the music and lyrics when it came to dealing with her feelings of grief and despair. Both Mavis and Matt believed that it didn't matter what pulled her through, as long as it was a positive way of expression and didn't drive her to do anything violent or unacceptable. The music seemed to be doing that, and everyone in Kim's life who cared about her was relieved.

She also seemed to have put Shanice Hall out of her mind the way her two friends had. Kim now seemed determined to have a good time no matter what. Even while they practiced Kenpo and broke a sweat, Kim seemed eager to enjoy even her mistakes, and she cracked several jokes regarding those of herself and her friends. Mavis, especially, understood that Kim had been torn apart by Shawn's loss, and now she was beginning to see the light at the end of the tunnel for her friend. It gave her a feeling of deep-seated happiness and satisfaction.

Matt and Kim both had supper with Mavis and her parents and followed it up by watching two classic horror zombie flicks as a family. Most of the scenes in the movies were almost laughable, because of the age of the filming and scripts, but mostly because Mavis knew what she was, and both movies seemed to play on mere suspicions of what being a zombie would be like. The three kids and Jane and Todd alike got big kicks out of the pictures, but deep inside, both Mavis and Matt knew that there was a shred of truth to the fiction they were watching. The murderous and conniving Shanice had turned out to be proof of that.

Mavis' friends left for home at 11:30, with Matt driving Kim home as usual, or what had become normal since Shawn's passing, anyway. Mavis' mother made her a late night "blood shake," a creation she had come up with on her own that included both blood and brains. It ended up looking a lot like there were raspberries somewhere in it, but only Mavis and her mom knew that the treat was about as un-vegan as it could get. Together, they sat at the table until nearly one in the morning, Mavis with her blood shake, and Jane with her root beer float, and they talked about where the three friends were at in their minds with the prom.

"So," Jane began when they first sat down with their glasses, "you're all feeling okay about the dance, right Mav?"

Mavis finished a long suck off her straw, nodding as she did so. "Believe it or not, I don't think any of us could be in a better state of mind. All three of us are excited, Mom... even Kim. She says she wants to have fun, and I'm genuinely hoping that she can maybe meet someone new to spark her interest."

Jane nodded. "Just keep in mind that the kind of pain Kim is feeling will likely last the rest of her life; it will never leave. She will only learn to live with it. Patience is the most important gift you can give her right now, dear."

Mavis took another long draw on her straw and thought about her mother's words. "You mean, no matter how much time passes, this is going to stick with her?"

Jane was silent for a moment, then looked up at her daughter with a sad look in her eyes. "Can I tell you a story?"

Mavis met her eyes and nodded, then whispered,

"Of course."

Jane was smiling, but it was a smile filled with longing and past memories, both sadness and the joy of knowing whatever it was she knew. "Long before I met your father, maybe in the third grade, I had a best friend. Now, keep in mind that I didn't get involved with Todd until our sophomore year in high school. Anyway, in the third grade, I had a best friend... his name was Kevin Klinger, and our mothers were best friends. He moved here from Seattle that school year; and our teacher sat him right next to me, then she assigned me to be his buddy for his first week."

Jane got a bit misty-eyed, and her slight smile began to tinge with pain. Mavis waited patiently for her to continue, to tell her the rest of the story, but she had a sinking feeling that the ending wasn't going to be good. After several moments passed, Jane continued.

"Kevin was funny," she said. "Even at that age, he had a quick wit and sense of humor that bordered on being adult-like. Oh, we used to laugh at anything and everything, but that was only the beginning. Kevin was adorable... easily the cutest boy at Greenville Elementary, and all of the girls had a crush on him. But the surprising thing was that Kevin had no interest in anyone but me. I was sure that we were just the best of friends, but by the end of the fourth-grade year, Kevin straightened me out."

"What do you mean?" Mavis was all wrapped up in the story, and her mother had just begun.

"Well, on the very last day of school, after we had

been let out for the summer, Kevin and I went for a short hike up to the Pointe."

Mavis got a shocked look on her face; what did a couple of nine- or ten-year-old kids expect to do at the Pointe, a place where high-schoolers and young adults worked on coming of age? She was flabbergasted at what her mother was telling her, and Jane caught on to her daughter's shock right away.

"Don't worry, Mavis," she said with a chuckle. "Back then the Pointe was nothing more than trails that led to the peak of a grassy hill. All the neighborhood kids frequented it, hiking and hanging out, building forts and the like. Kevin and I were no different, and we even had a fort of our own that we had built with our own hands, just the two of us."

Mavis breathed a sigh of relief, and Jane continued.

"So, we went to the top of the Pointe, to our fort, and there we were jabbering about being done with fourth-grade, and what fifth would be like. That was when I told him about a message that a classmate had given me to pass on to him. Her name was Donna Morris, and she was the richest, most popular girl around at the time."

Mavis waited impatiently for her to continue, then finally lost it and asked anxiously, "So? What was the message?"

Jane didn't skip a beat. "She liked Kevin very much, and she wanted to be his girlfriend. It pained me to talk to him about it because I thought I was in love with him myself. I had high hopes, but as far as I knew, he thought we were just friends, and I wouldn't ruin that by admitting my feelings. So, I passed on Donna's message."

"What did he say?"

Jane smiled again and looked out the sliding glass doors into the darkness that shrouded the backyard. "He laughed. He said, 'That phony? That phony is made of plastic! I could never have a girlfriend like that. Besides,' he said… 'I want a girlfriend like you. Why don't you be my girlfriend?' "

Her voice cracked when she repeated his words, but Jane maintained control. "From that moment forward, at least until the end, I was."

Mavis searched her mother's face. "The… end?"

Jane nodded, and the tears slowly began to come. "One day in seventh grade, Kevin missed the school bus. I stalled the driver as long as I could, but finally, I had to get on and go with the rest of the students. Kevin never showed up to school that day. In fact, he never showed up to school again." She quickly stood up and grabbed a tissue from the box on the edge of the counter. Wiping her eyes and blowing her nose seemed to take forever.

"What happened?" Mavis asked. "Did he get sick?"

Jane blew again, then shook her head, a look of torment on her face. "No. He had been walking to the bus stop that morning, just like usual, but disappeared, in thin air, before he got there… like a puff of smoke. They found his body nine days later at the base of the Pointe, thrown into some brush, naked and… well, you know. Kevin Klinger had been abducted and murdered." She looked her daughter dead in the eye then. "My point is, that happened in seventh-grade; we had been 'in love' since the end of fourth, or longer. By the time he was murdered, both of us were planning our wedding; we planned to marry each other, as soon as we graduated, and we meant it. But it was never meant to be."

Mavis didn't know what to say. She sat before her mother, the blood shake forgotten in front of her, getting warm. As she let the story she had just been told sink into her soul, she had a thousand thoughts running through her mind. Only one, however, was able to find its way to her lips and out into the open.

"But you're over it, right Mom," she asked in a low voice. "I mean, that was a very long time ago; surely you don't even think about it much anymore."

Jane turned to her daughter, so naïve and innocent, and replied, "There isn't a day that goes by that I don't think about Kevin Klinger, Mavis. Even if it's only for a fleeting second. That's why I get it… that's why I know how Kim is feeling, and that's also why I don't expect her to ever really get over what she has been through regarding Shawn."

Her mother paused for a second, then turned back to Mavis. "That's not to say she won't find love; I guarantee that she will. But she will never be the same, and she will never forget him. It will take her a while to adjust to the pain, but that's all she will be able to do. The pain doesn't go away… you just learn to live with it, because it is now a part of you. It will play an integral part in the girl she now is, and the woman she is to become."

"Um, Mother, I don't understand why you haven't reached out to Kim to share this." Mavis' voice sounded both mildly disgusted and slightly impatient. "I mean, this could really help her, really give her hope and a deeper understanding of her personal power in dealing with this. But you've kept it to yourself, and I guess that's a bit disappointing to me."

Jane stared at Mavis for a bit, a look of confusion on her face at first, as she digested her daughter's somewhat-harsh words. Slowly, however, her eyes softened, and a slight look of guilt came over her face. Mavis knew immediately that even Jane was wondering why she hadn't reached out to the girl she had known for so many years. It wasn't like Kim was a stranger; in fact, in many ways, Kim was like a daughter to her.

"I've been selfish," she finally said. "I didn't want to share that part of me with anyone. If you want to know the truth, your father doesn't even know the whole story; I told him Kevin, and I broke up before it happened, and that I was over him."

"Well, Mom, it's not too late." Mavis leaned forward, sliding her shake out of the way slightly as she did so. "Kim is coming tomorrow to go with me for hair and manicures. She's going to get ready here. What if I have her come a bit early, and then when she gets here, I'll pretend that I'm running late. I could stay out of the way while you talk to her." Jane had a very apprehensive look on her face, which Mavis immediately caught. "I'm telling you, you could help her more in twenty minutes than any of us have been able to in months. Mom, it would be criminal and wrong not to do this."

Jane took a deep breath. "Fine. Fine, I'll do it."

Mavis jumped up from the table with her shake in hand to deposit in the sink. She stopped and embraced her mother long and hard, the little warmth she had in her heart reaching out through her chest and grabbing her mother's own beating one. For a second, they both felt more love from each other than they had in a very long time.

Letting go of Jane, she looked her in the eye and whispered, "Thank you so much, Mommy."

Jane burst out laughing at the term, and Mavis followed right away. The next thing they knew Todd was yelling from his bedroom door for them to keep quiet, or better yet, get their butts to bed. This made them laugh even more, but soon they resigned themselves to the fact that the day was over, and tomorrow would demand much… from both of them. The two said their goodnights, hugged yet again and went their separate ways.

Mavis lay in bed that Friday night thinking about Kevin Klinger. She found herself wondering what kind of human being took children and harmed them in such ways. She cried for the dead youth, without tears of course, then she cried for her mother.

It was then that a single, salty tear found its way

down her cheek, and finally, she was able to sleep, relieved that she had released a single drop.

CHAPTER 27

Mavis woke on Saturday morning around 7:30, the sun streaming through the open shades of her window, lighting up her pale face with a warmth that she wished she felt more often. For twenty minutes, she lay there, still and smiling, enjoying the blessing of the sun on this fine Saturday, the day of her senior prom.

At nearly eight she picked up her cell phone and dialed Kim, who answered on the second ring.

"Hey, you!" Kim greeted enthusiastically. "I knew you would be calling me bright and early. Believe me, I barely got any sleep last night, I'm so excited. I have a good feeling about tonight; I think I might actually have a bit of fun."

"You will," Mavis replied, smiling. "Listen, what time were you planning to get here to take off to the salon?"

"Around eleven. I figured we could grab an early lunch before we hit the parlor."

Mavis paused, recalling her mother's tale from the night before. "Well, I wondered if you would be willing to come around ten. I was hoping to get a bit of an earlier start. Do you mind? I mean, you don't have anything else to do, right?"

Kim thought about it. "No, I don't. Why, what's going on?"

Mavis could tell she was suspicious for some reason, but Kim was suspicious a lot nowadays. "No, nothing special, I just wanted some company while I figured out for sure what I was going to have done with my hair."

Kim hesitated. "I thought you chose a 'do.'"

"Well, I changed my mind, and now I'm unsure." Mavis was getting frustrated with her friend. "Look, are you going to come a little early, or not?"

"Sure, sure, Mavis." Kim coughed. "I'll be there by ten-thirty, if not ten, okay?"

"Good, see you then."

The girls hung up, and Mavis quickly got out of bed to find out what her mother had to feed her. Stomach growling, she made her way out of the room. As soon as she stepped into the hall, she could smell fresh blood, and she knew that Jane had hooked her up well. She reached the table to see a plateful of gory chicken innards with a bowl of raw eggs alongside it. Mavis beamed and looked over at her mother, who stuck her tongue out and rolled her eyes as she filled her coffee cup.

"I don't think I'll ever get used to your diet," Jane said, "but my love for you overlooks the situation quite well."

Mavis grabbed a straw from a package in the cupboard.

"What's that for?" Jane asked.

Mavis grinned. "I have to eat the eggs with something, right?"

Sitting down at the table, she began to get situated. "So, I spoke to Kim this morning, and she's going to be early. It was obvious to me that she thinks something is up, but I tried to act as normal as possible. As soon as she gets here, I'm heading to my room, so you answer the door and take it from there, Mom."

Jane groaned. "What will I say?"

Mavis shrugged and swallowed a bite of the innards. "Just bring her in here, offer her something, and start talking. You're the best at it; I mean, at being... relatable and gentle. Just follow your heart. If she asks what I'm doing, just tell her I'm going through some jewelry, in case I decide on different accessories. Tell her you asked me to let the two of you be alone."

With a deep breath, her mother replied, "Fine."

It didn't take Mavis long to inhale her breakfast. She sat at the table drinking the milk her mother insisted upon and making conversation about the dance, but they didn't have much time to talk at all. The doorbell rang about a half-hour before Mavis expected, so with a wink at Jane, she got up and bolted for her bedroom. Just as she got the door shut and locked the door, she could hear Kim's voice greeting "Mrs. Harvey," and she heard Jane invite her best friend in and tell her a line about what Mavis was doing, and wouldn't she like a donut while she waited?

While the two talked, Mavis made her bed while listening to some heavy music, then laid out her prom dress and accessories on top of it. The dress was faux black leather, and she couldn't have been more pleased with the entire get-up. After gazing endlessly at the outfit and considering how Matt would look in his clothing at her side, she turned to her desk and got on her laptop; she wanted to see if she could find more goth-like formal hairstyles for the affair. She was hoping that perhaps something more dramatic would catch her eye than what she had already opted for.

After about forty-five minutes went by, there was a light knock on her door.

"Mav? It's me, Kim."

Her voice sounded weak and light, and Mavis knew that Jane's story had some kind of effect on her friend. She jumped up from her desk and rushed to the door, unlocking it and swinging it open. Kim walked in, red-eyed and smiling. As Mavis closed the door behind her, Kim made her way to the beanbag chair and plopped down.

"You know," she began, "if you had told me that your mom wanted to talk, I would have come over anyway. You acted like it was a big secret or something."

"No, I didn't," Mavis replied. "I just lied." She turned to her friend and sat down at the desk again. "My mom never told me the story she told you until last night, and all I could think was that perhaps it would help... you know, give you some kind of hope for the future."

Kim smiled and wiped a stray tear from the corner

of her eye. "It did. More than you could know. I have to admit, just knowing that someone close to me, someone who cares for me, has gone through something almost identical makes me feel like I'm not alone in the world and that maybe life really will go on."

"It will."

Kim continued as if she didn't hear her friend. "I mean, look at her and Todd, so happy and in love, and for as long as I've known them. I can't help but have hope, you know what I mean?"

Mavis nodded and smiled, but it was time to change the subject and move on; they were running out of time for their salon appointments. "Remember what 'do' I was going to have done? Well, what do you think of this one instead?"

The new style consisted of pure white on one side, and black on the other. Mavis' hair was waist length by this time so it would be incredible-looking. Also, it had a bit of a light curl to the long tresses, giving it a soft appearance. Kim's face lit up as soon as she saw it.

"I love it," she said.

Mavis nodded. "So do I. Do you have your mom's credit card? I do, and I'm ready."

Kim glanced at the clock radio. "I am too, so let's hit it, girl."

Grabbing their purses, the two left the room, stopping only long enough to tell Jane they were heading out for their makeovers. She let her mom know they would be home by two, gave her a quick kiss and hug, which Kim did as well, and then they were out the door like a flash.

They ended up stopping at Sports Burger and going through the drive-thru for lunch, which Mavis ordered but only picked through in the salon parking lot. The breakfast Jane gave her had satisfied her beyond belief, and she thought it might be her new favorite, at least for the time being. Kim scarfed down her food, and even when they were both done, they had fifteen minutes to spare before their appointments.

They were using a new salon called "Up and Combing," and they had heard many good things about the girls that worked there. With photos in hand of what they wanted, including printed pics of the manicures they had chosen, it was going to be an expensive outing, but it always was when it came to school dances. This one was special, however, and both of their mothers had told them to spare no expense. Both Mavis and Kim knew how blessed they were to have the parents they had.

So, they spent hours getting their hair done, then their manicures and pedicures. They laughed, drank cappuccinos, and gossiped with the stylists, who were enjoying the time as much as the girls were. Lastly, they had their makeup done, which their salon artists gave them advice on so they could touch it up properly right before the dance, and for maintenance during. They even gave each girl a sheet of instructions for the makeup so they couldn't really mess it up if they tried. Mavis and Kim were so pleased with it all that they tipped the girls extravagantly and promised that they would be using "Up and Combing" on a regular basis.

By the time they left the salon, it was nearly four. Not wanting to waste any more time, they swung by Matt's to see where he stood on getting ready. He ended up acting like getting ready was the last thing he was worried about in the world, as they found him mowing the family lawn. Mavis interrupted him long enough to get him to drive them back to her house so he could keep the convertible; he would be picking them up, and she didn't want him to show up in his beat up old car, so she made an exception for his appearance sake.

As for Jane, she oohed and aahed over Kim's look, and pretty much did the same for Mavis, though she could see that her mother was faking some of it. She understood. Black and white were a bit stark for anyone, especially a mother whose daughter was attending her last high school prom, but Jane pulled off looking impressed very well. It made Mavis smile, and she gave her mom a big hug for good measure.

They had a light supper, with Kim joining in since there would be an abundance of food at the dance. After that, it was nearly five, and they needed to focus on getting ready. The girls excused themselves to Mavis' bedroom where they began to prepare themselves for the biggest day of the senior year, next to graduation, of course.

While they dressed, they listened to music, told jokes, and laughed. Maintaining a cheerful mood was imperative, and they were determined to do so. Because of that, they found themselves having the time of their lives together for the first time in a long time.

Shanice Hall was the furthest thing from their minds.

CHAPTER 28

Melanna and Dalton sat stiffly in their formal wear, waiting in their hotel room with drinks in their hands, waiting in silence for Shanice to make her grand appearance through the adjoining door. She had gone out earlier in the day and driven the rental to Cleveland, where she had her hair and nails done. She had dyed her hair a stark red, almost fire-engine in color; her makeup white, except for the dark and dramatic eyes and lip color. Her nails came to a violent point and were blood red. Both of her minions thought she looked magnificent.

They didn't look so wonderful, however, though they did look very good. Dalton wore a navy and gray tux, while Melanna wore a gray job with lots of navy lace. She kept her hair long, only pulling it back on the side with clips adorned with black widow spiders. Dalton's long, curly hair was simply washed, doused in mousse, and shaken free. They looked good, but their leader promised to look breathtaking.

By the time she was finished, it was eight in the evening; the prom was already in full swing, but that didn't matter. She had informed her tiny crew that they would make their appearance at ten sharp. By then, pretty much everyone would be walking out of the Westside gymnasium. It would be the perfect opportunity for them to make a spectacle out of Mavis and her own small crew.

She also insisted that, no matter how wonderful the humans smelled, no matter how delectable they looked, there was to be absolutely no eating or attacks at the senior prom. They were going for one purpose and one purpose only: to humiliate and threaten her enemy. From there they would take one of her friends for supper, and that they would enjoy on the road, as they would be going right from the dance to the airport to catch a plane back to Montego Bay. They would have to change clothing in the car on the way, lest they could be identified at the airport, but Shanice didn't worry about such things. Her plans were always perfect.

The door that joined their rooms flew open suddenly, and Shanice stood there in a tight green bodice dress that complemented her red locks beautifully. Her hands were on her hips, a smile on her face, and she turned in small, slow circles as she let them cast their eyes upon the perfection that was she.

"Well?"

Melanna was the first to respond. "You are breathtaking, my Queen."

Shanice smiled her approval and turned her gaze to Dalton.

"You're perfect," he whispered.

"I know," she replied. "This is going to be a very

good night, my loves... a very good night indeed. For now, let's have a bit of brain hors d'oeuvres I saved for us. We won't be able to eat at the dance, of course, and it will be a while before we enjoy our victim on the way to the plane. Oh, and eat delicately... I want no blood or tissue on these clothes, got it?"

The three of them set about their little snack, and it wasn't long before they were washing off their hands and faces, touching up makeup, and fixing their hairstyles, returning them to perfection. By the time the last of the lipstick had been applied to the lips of Shanice and Melanna, it was time to take-off.

"You will stand behind me, parallel, one on my right, one on my left. Your hands will be clasped behind your backs, and you will smile with only half of your lips. Your eyes will be steely, set, and somber, and neither of you will speak a word unless I speak to you first. These are the rules, and this is the plan; do you comprehend completely?"

Again, in stereo: "Of course."

"I say we have a couple of drinks in my room," Shanice said lightly as she adjusted the tight skirt of her green formal. "After that, it will be just about time to set out for the dance... and for Mavis."

They retreated into her room, closing the door to their own, and while Dalton sat in a chair and Shanice partially and stiffly lounged on the bed, Melanna mixed drinks. Shanice flipped on the clock radio and lowered the sound, then moaned as she grasped her drink out of Melanna's offering hand and sipped long and hard through the thin straw inside.

"Perfect," she purred.

∞

Westside High School Gymnasium; 6:50 PM

Matt with money for three tickets in hand, Mavis, and Kim stood in the line leading to the Westside High School senior prom in the gymnasium. Tickets were being sold to those who didn't reserve at the very head of the line, and admission was also taking place there as well. Mavis had insisted that Matt pay (with Mavis paying for Kim) so that he would look like the ultimate gentleman. He appreciated it, and even through his pasty face makeup, she could see his light blush.

The level of noise and laughter was staggering, but they got through it by making their own brand of noise through personal conversation. Yes, they practically had to yell to get their points across, but they didn't mind. The three of them were having a great time in that sweaty, hot line, and they hadn't even made it inside the gym yet.

Regardless of the seeming drudgery of movement, slowly but surely, they were advancing. By 7:20, twenty full minutes after the actual event had begun, Matt found himself purchasing three tickets after they had shown their student IDs, of course. As if the greatest waste of money in the world for twenty-five dollars per ticket, the "ticket usher" (Mr. Canton, the Life Skills instructor) snatched them from his hand, tore them in half, tossed them into a wastepaper basket that was overflowing, and stamped them on the hand with a bold, black "WW", for Westside Wasps. Matt glanced back at Mavis and Kim, and all of them burst out laughing, to which Mr. Canton replied with a wrinkling of his nose as if he smelled something bad. Quickly, they passed through the threshold and into the gym.

The gym seemed massive, all cleared out. On the stage at the far end was a local school band who called themselves "The Senior Smashers," and they were doing an incredibly bad rendition of a heavy metal song. Surprisingly, the thrill of the event made them sound good, and no one seemed to take notice of their amateur status at all.

The room was darker than Mavis remembered it the year before, but that was because she was focused more on food than fun at that time. Tonight she was wearing an abundance of vapor rub, but she had pretty much globbed it up inside of her nostrils in order to save her makeup. All three of them were marinated in perfume and cologne. To be honest, it was working a thousand times better that way; she couldn't smell a thing except for eucalyptus, and it made her very happy.

Disco balls spun, strobe lights flickered, and kids danced and talked all around them. After a long moment, Matt and Kim formed a small circle around Mavis and got her attention away from all the sparkle and flair. It took them a minute; she seemed to be entranced by her surroundings.

"Mavis," Matt began, his voice yelling over the din. "Hey! Mavis, are you okay?" When she still didn't respond, Kim reached out and grabbed her by the arm, giving it a good, stiff shake.

Suddenly, she jerked back to reality and turned to her friends, giving both of them a gleaming smile. "What?"

"Are you okay?" Matt asked again. "I mean, are you in control?"

Mavis laughed. "This is amazing! Yes! I'm in control! I put that gloop right up my nose tonight, and it's like I'm actually enjoying the world. Look at the lights, listen to the music! Look! Check out Dexter dancing by himself. Oh, this is great!"

Both Matt and Kim sighed with relief after exchanging looks. "Okay," Matt continued, "What do you want to do first? Dance?"

Mavis laughed again. "Dance? Ha! First, we have to get a partner for Kim. Until then, I say we eat!"

Now it was her friends' turn to laugh. "Fine." He grabbed Mavis by the hand and Kim, gently, by the arm, and steered them to the long buffet table against the east wall of the gym.

It took them a while to get there for a number of reasons. There was the crowd, then they had the number of students, and teachers alike, that stopped them talking as they struggled for the sustenance. By the time they finally got to the buffet, it was only five minutes until eight.

The bands switched to an ancient classic rock song, which was still a goody, and Mavis started to dance in place as she piled sliced ham, roast beef, turkey, and salami onto her paper plate. She also grabbed some cold fried chicken, and bacon wrapped asparagus, which both Matt and Kim were sure she was going to eat. At the very end of the line, she took a cup of punch, then turned around and stood impatiently, foot tapping, while her two friends rushed to fill their plates with just about everything she didn't have.

"Oh, good" she groaned as they finally made their way to her. "You'd think you guys just had a big dinner or something! C'mon… let's find somewhere to sit. I'm dying here."

It was easy enough to find a small table that held the three of them. Most of the other attendees were either dancing or mingling. Only a few of them were going through the line, and then it was only to grab a single thing or two and then go back to their dates or friends. As soon as they sat, Mavis dug in like a madwoman, bringing smiles to the faces of her companions. At one point she looked up to see them both staring and smiling, and she stopped in her tracks.

"What?"

Kim and Matt burst out laughing.

"Nothing, Mav," Matt reassured. "You're just awesome, that's all."

"Huh," she muttered. "Funny."

Without a second thought, Mavis dove back into her plate, and they took that as a sign that they, too, needed to hit the food. The band's loud music was tempting the three of them to get up and dance, and that wasn't going to happen until Mavis had at least fooled her appetite. A glance at her plate told them both it wouldn't be long, and they had better get on the ball.

Two minutes after they started eating, Mavis stopped and wiped her mouth. With an excited smile, she looked at them both, and her smile slowly faded. They were both still eating; she couldn't believe it! She was just getting ready to open her mouth and give them the business for taking so long, but suddenly someone approached their table and stopped. The three of them looked up, tense with preparation at who it might be. Then they saw that it was Tony Clark, a popular, good-looking boy who was involved in every sport at Westside.

"Hi, Tony," Matt greeted, holding out his hand to shake. "What's happening?"

"Not much," Tony hollered over the noise. "Just doing the prom. Did you two know you're up for king and queen?"

Mavis froze. "Who?"

Tony laughed. "You! You and Morgan here."

The two shot each other a glance. "No, we had no idea." Matt seemed a bit stricken, and Mavis thought she might die. "Um, can't we opt out?"

Tony shook his head. "Naw," he yelled. "Voting has already begun. As a matter of fact, that little metal pot in the middle of the table has the ballots. You need to vote and drop it in the box up by the stage. Ain't the music awesome?"

They all nodded.

Tony's big brown eyes shifted to Kim. "Hey, Kim.

You look amazing." It was strange to hear the compliment being hollered. "So, um… do you want to dance with me?"

Kim's eyes went directly to Mavis, who smiled. She shifted them back to Tony and flashed her best smile. "You know," she replied thoughtfully. "I'd like that, Tony… I'd really, really like that."

Tony Clark held out his hand and took Kim's, and he slowly and considerately led her to the dance floor. Mavis and Matt watched until they disappeared into the crowd, then turned their attention to each other. Matt reached out and took Mavis by the hand.

"Shall we?" he asked.

Mavis gave him a vigorous nod in return. "But first, I think we ought to vote for anyone but ourselves to be Westside Royalty."

Matt laughed hard. "Yes ma'am… I agree."

With that, they both grabbed a ballot and pencil and made their vote. When they were done, they folded the slips of paper in half and put the pencils back. Mavis gave Matt a stern look.

"Don't forget to remind Kim, will you?" she asked.

∞

The minutes which filled the hours that made up the Westside High senior prom passed by faster than anything Mavis had ever endured. They ate, they danced like mad, made jokes, mingled, and even socialized with the teachers and chaperones, chatting about the plans they had for their futures.

Kim spent the rest of the night with Tony Clark. Not in a clingy way, but in a comfortable, almost "friends for life" kind of way that made Mavis believe in the future. Several times, the pair joined Mavis and Matt, but mostly, they did their own thing, and they did it well.

Suddenly, it all abruptly ended. The lead singer of the band stopped the music, excused his players, and announced that it was now time to induct the prom king and queen!

Mavis and Matt both froze and glanced at the large, cage-covered gym clock. It was nine-forty-five already... yes, it was time to announce the king and queen.

"We don't stand a chance," Mavis said close to his ear, so he could hear her. "Look at us, I mean."

Matt gave her a serious look. "I don't know, Mavis. I have a feeling..."

He couldn't finish his sentence. In the next second the principal was on stage, beaming with excitement and beginning his obligatory prom speech. Matt held Mavis' hand, and they waited in suspense, both hoping that things would turn out in a manner that didn't direct any attention toward them. Who had nominated them, anyway?

Suddenly, Mavis heard Kim's voice on her left shoulder. "No need to thank me for the nomination. You both deserve it, and I love you that much."

Mavis groaned... gosh, darn that Kim!

CHAPTER 29

Shanice Hall sat in the Westside High School parking lot, the one closest to the gym doors that let out to the football field. Students shuffled in and out, music blared, and laughter guffawed, all in seeming harmony. She rolled down the driver's side window of the rental and cleared her throat disgustingly.

"You don't like the music?"

Dalton's voice was beginning to feel like sandpaper on her eardrums. Her nerves were frazzled, not because of facing Mavis, but because of the fury, she felt at the fact that this girl was enjoying her life! Shanice should be the one dancing and being the center of attention. She should even be up for prom queen! Had she known that Mavis was, she may have lost her self-control altogether and tore through the school like a bone saw through a side of beef.

"It's not about the music, Dalton," she said as calmly as she could. "It's about the one person I hate being inside, enjoying it."

In her rearview mirror, she saw Melanna elbow Dalton hard and shoot him a look of disgust, a look that said: quiet! This is not about you! Dalton's hand came up to his arm and rubbed as if she had broken a bone. His face scrunched up in pain, and with a shake of her head, Shanice realized what a freaking moron Dalton really was. Melanna, on the other hand, seemed to have it all together.

Kids who had been sitting in cars suddenly left their vehicles and began to walk like soldiers down to the gym entrance. Shanice took immediate notice and rolled down her window. With a simple way of her tiny hand, she waved over one of the students to her window.

"What's going on? Why's everyone going in?" She asked.

The kid gave a giggle and said, "They're announcing the king and queen, the big sheep and his momma sheep, whatever. They're doin' the royalty thing, man."

Shanice could have puked on his patent leather shoes, but rather than risk harming her own dress, simply rolled up her window and turned her focus back to the double-gym doors.

Perfect, the prom will be over shortly.

∞

Principle Pearson beamed out at the students as he paused for effect during the short speech he was giving. There was a lot to talk about this year, or at least briefly mention. Mavis wanted to run, but Matt held her hand, smiled at her, and gave her the strength to stay with her head held high.

At last, after what seemed like an eternity, the principal tucked his speech card into his inner jacket pocket and went into the tradition of prom king and queen. How it began, or so his research told him, how it had evolved, and what it was like today at Westside High in Greenville as compared to other schools in the country. It seemed like an eternity until he got to the nominees.

"And so, without further ado, I, Principal Pearson of Greenville High, proudly announce the nominees for king and queen!"

The place exploded into screams, whistles, and applause that was deafening. Everyone had their hands over their ears, including the students making the most noise.

"The nominees are…"

Mr. Pearson was beginning to get into the thick of things, and soon the king and queen would be announced. The room got silent (or as silent as it possibly could), and the man continued.

"Maddie Johnson and Jacob Lee!"

The crowd went haywire as the pair made their way, blushing and shucking, to the stage area. Maddie kept trying to grab onto Jacob's hand, but he was so busy being a stud in front of his friends that he was missing her cues. She made up for it by rubbing his shoulder and smiling like some kind of beauty queen. Once they had taken their places on the tape X's, Mr. Pearson continued.

"Next up, we have Gabrielle Martin and Christopher Thompson! Come on up, kids!"

A near duplicate scene took place as the second pair

wove around and struggled to the stage. Mavis suddenly remembered Kim and tried to steal a glance in her direction; she caught just enough of a look to see the girl was having a good time. Her friends stared straight ahead.

"Now we come to the third pair of nominees, a couple I would refer to as something of a surprise, but very deserving of the titles nonetheless." Mr. Pearson cleared his throat and beamed. "Mavis Harvey and Matthew Morgan!"

Now the entire gymnasium went off the deep-end. Mavis suddenly felt boxed in; every student in her proximity gather around her, and it was only by means of a small slit between people, she could make it to the stage. She climbed the three short steps to the stage and turned around to address the gym. The madness continued while Mavis stood on her 'X,' struggling just to catch her breath. It felt almost like a dream, a hallucination, she felt Matt put his arm around her and hug her close. She looked up into his smiling eyes, and her anxiety ebbed.

"The second runners-up, who will enjoy a one-day getaway at Crazyland Park this summer… Christopher Thompson and Gabrielle Martin!"

Mr. Pearson was giving the winning envelope to the second runners-up, Gabrielle and Chris… the envelope with the tickets to Crazyland.

"And now, one of the most 'edge-of-your-seat' moments of every year, I will announce the first runners-up, which, inevitably, will reveal the new king and queen. Please continue to give your attention to the first runners-up and the giving of their prize, seniors!"

Pearson cleared his throat and put his eyes on the card once again. "The first runners-up of the senior prom, who will enjoy $250 toward their first year's college tuition: Jacob Lee and Maddie Johnson!"

Mavis felt the world almost fall completely apart around her. She could hear nothing but the sound of the white noise coming from all the students, especially those who were trying to break into her space, seemingly all at once.

Pearson raised his voice into the microphone. "Our new King and Queen are Mavis Harvey and Matthew Morgan." Mr. Pearson was surrounded with kids and struggling to hand Mavis flowers and the winning envelope with $500 toward their first year's college tuition. Instantly, Matt surrounded her with his arms and pushed everyone away, as he kissed Mavis deeply and continued to spin her around. Mavis was in heaven.

CHAPTER 30

That was when Shanice noticed the changes that had taken place. There had been chaperones, two men, one on each side of the double doors. They were gone now. Students who had been loitering outside or hanging in cars were now herding themselves out those same double doors. Now was the time to go. Now was the time to get into position outside the Westside senior prom. She couldn't care less about the crowning of whatever king and queen there would be; Shanice just wanted to get at Mavis with her minions, and this appeared to be the only chance she would have.

"Both of you!" she shouted sharply to Melanna and Dalton, but mostly to Melanna. "Now is the time, follow me, hold your directed stances, do not flinch, but hold yourselves steady at all times. No questions! Let's go!"

Like magic, Shanice, Melanna, and Dalton got out of the rental and melded into the ever-moving line that was flowing out of the gymnasium. Shanice initiated a light conversation, directed at Melanna only, and it made them look like they belonged there even more.

It wasn't ten minutes and Shanice Hall, along with

her minions, was standing only thirty feet from the Westside gymnasium doors. Shanice in the front, her sidekicks to each side of her rear, all smiles and rear-clasped hands. Shanice was ready for anything, and therefore, so were Melanna and Dalton.

Now, all they needed was Mavis to exit for the perfect moment so it would be unforgettable.

∞

The gym was clearing out fast. Mr. Pearson retreated backstage as quickly as he could, as though deserting troops at war. Just like that, the senior prom was all over. Slowly, but surely, the noise died down. Tony gave Kim a kiss as they said their goodnights. Mavis and Matt waved at Tony as Kim approached. Kim said with a sad look on her face, "He has to work. Well, let's go." The three turned and headed for the door.

The prom dwindled slowly, from a roar too loud talking to mumbles, to the occasional laugh or sneeze; the place was emptying out.

Everyone, that is, except for Shanice, Dalton, and Melanna, who all stood erect, in proper silence, waiting patiently outside for that ever elusive "right moment."

Shanice shifted her eyes from here to there, searching for Mavis. She glanced nonchalantly around the crowd, but for the life of her could not spot the pitch-black, paper-straight hair that Mavis had sported the last time she had visited Greenville. Yet she was convinced that was what she was to be searching for.

However, while Shanice was unaware of where

Mavis was, Mavis had caught on to something amiss with the trio only twenty feet away from where she stood. One was a vibrant redhead with her hair worn up; it fell in tiny curls around her white face, and her makeup, including her blusher, eyeshadow, and lipstick, were in the same green that her dress sported. The other two were in gray with black lace trim.

Mavis didn't recognize any of them, per se. What caught her attention about them, even in the middle of the madness, was a simple fact that those three displayed no madness. They stood, poker straight, and stared. On several occasions, Mavis could have sworn that the ginger's eyes were shifting to and fro, but there was so much action happening between them that she couldn't get a good, dependable look at her.

But then there was the smell.

Sure, Mavis' use of the vapor rub drowned out the smell of others. Yes, it kept her from giving in to her temptations. But when she had worn it during the field trip to the hospital, it had done nothing to stifle the smell of the truly dead. It was a smell that, to her, had no competition; it seeped into her mouth.

She could taste it, in spades.

"I think Shanice is here," alerting her friends.

As the parking lot quickly cleared out, leaving only stragglers, that was when it happened.

"Mavis! Mavis Harvey!"

That's when she saw the red-haired girl's face turn as red as her hair. Even then, she was caught up in the moment, and concern slipped from her grasp.

From where Mavis was standing, she could see the red-head in the green dress, staring at her and pointing a sharp blood red nail in her direction. Fire flared in her eyes, and it was that fire that brought full recognition of who was confronting her. She was facing and looking into the fiery eyes of Shanice Hall, red hair or not.

Everyone had been looking for the murderous monster for so long, and suddenly, there she was right in front of them.

Now they had a firm grasp on how she was managing to live the high life, partying and traveling around freely without a care.

"So, first you steal my life, then you steal my crown. You are no more a queen than the wimpy little girl in the bathroom that you tried to save so many months ago." Shanice began to walk forward toward Mavis with long strides, her two minions right behind her, not missing a stride or step.

"Are you frightened, little Miss Harvey?" Shanice began to laugh heartily, and her sidekicks followed suit. "Well, I wouldn't worry tonight. I simply wanted to surprise you and your measly little mortal friends."

Students and staff were hysterical and trying to save their own lives. Cars flew out of the field and off school property right and left.

"Don't worry, kiddies!" she screamed as she ran her sharp finger across the parking lot as though addressing every last person. "This isn't about you… not yet. But eventually, it will be about you all. You act frightened of me, yet you don't even know who you live around, attend classes with, and mingle with. You have no understanding of what Mavis Harvey has done." She whirled to look at Mavis, her finger pointing at her dead on. "But I know, Mavis, and I will keep your secret... all the way until I feast on the brains of your ignorant friends."

Ever since she had been talking, Kim Coleman had been creeping stealthily and with rage, all the way around the cars. She took her position behind the female in the gray and black, Shanice's lackey, who now stood at one side of her while her muscular partner stood on the other. Their backs were to Kim, and they were facing Mavis only, their eyes glued to her face.

Matt watched as Kim continued to sneak until she was right up behind Melanna. She knew that the poor soul had been overcome with the evil that lived inside of Shanice Hall. Kim Coleman didn't even have to think about it.

In the blink of an eye, she screamed with a fury that made their skin crawl. Taking a single leap into the air, she executed a full roundhouse kick, and with one spike-heeled foot, she connected with Melanna's head. The result was chaos.

At the exact moment, Melanna's head had Kim's spiked heel sticking out of her forehead, her dead corpse went limp and fell to the ground. Kim removed her second heel and thrust towards Dalton. Matthew ran forward, knelt before Dalton, and threw a punch right at the bulky man's throat. His fist went all the way in his thick neck, stunning the guy. Black goo oozed around Matt's fist, and he had no choice but to grab the man's hair at the back of his head. Simultaneously, Kim connected with Dalton's body; Matt pulled one way, and Kim pushed the other way, tearing his melon clean off. Completely grossed out, Matt threw the head as far as he could toward the football field, sending it sailing. Dalton's corpse tumbled to the ground.

Mavis was frozen in place, her eyes roaming rapidly to and fro as she sought out the red-headed Shanice in the bright green dress. But even with the distinctive color, Mavis couldn't spot her. It appeared that Shanice had gone up in a puff of smoke, disappearing in the salvation of the chaos.

In less than four minutes flat, the parking lot was completely empty, except for Mavis, Matt, Kim, Melanna's body, and Dalton's body and distant head.

"Where did Shanice go?"

Mavis was breathing hard, and she was poised for immediate action, as were her friends. Matt was about five feet from her, and Kim was on the ground, still very near the eradicated Melanna. All of them held positions they had learned in Kenpo.

"I don't know," Kim panted as she turned circles, her eyes insane as she looked. "I saw her jump on a car, and then she was gone. Just like that, Mav… she was gone."

"Matt?"

He stood there, vigilant as he gasped for breath. "All I saw was the big guy, and I knew he was with her by the way he was staring at me… he must have been assigned to me or something. That was freaking crazy!"

"Well, she's somewhere, I tell ya!" Mavis was halfway between panic and rage. She heard the revving of a car engine and turned toward it.

Searching the few remaining cars, there… a lone, ugly, half-rusty sedan; leaning out of the window was a girl with bright red hair, a green dress, and fire in her eyes.

While the ignition ran and the headlights blinded, Shanice got out of the car, then climbed on the hood in her green heels, scratching the paint without care. She took steps back and forth across the hood, scratching and screeching, and smiling at the sound.

While Shanice entertained herself in that manner, the three of them instantly scattered and ducked behind different cars. Watching her act, Mavis got an idea. She whistled lightly, just enough to get the attention of her friends. With her right hand, and while Shanice was pacing and gazing at the sky, Mavis motioned that she was going to go out and around the building, to the back of Shanice's car. Matt made sure Shanice wasn't looking before turning back to tell Mavis, "No! Let me go!"

But Mavis was already gone.

"Come on out here, Tricky Trio!" Shanice's voice was a shrill scream. She stopped pacing and pointed her finger in the direction where Mavis was. "You took my family, now I think it's only fair that I take yours, Mavis Harvey! Come out, come out, wherever you are!"

Suddenly, both Matt and Kim saw Mavis. She was

coming up behind Shanice, slowly, and barefoot. She was almost strutting, her strides long and leisurely. As she got closer, they could see that she was smiling.

As if on cue Kim and Matt then stood up from behind the cars.

A look came over Shanice's face, out of the blue, like she had eaten something bad. She began to sniff the air, then spun around on the hood with a horrible screech. Matt and Kim crept toward Shanice quietly, so to keep her from turning around and attacking them. Matt thought about the look that had come over her face; she had looked scared to death. Was Shanice Hall not all she had cracked herself up to be?

"Mavis!" Suddenly her voice was as sweet as candy. She leaped off the hood of the car and landed clumsily on her dead feet, then gained her composure. "I just want to prepare you for the damage I am going to do in your life... the damage to come."

"There will be no damage," Mavis whispered as she took her place directly in front of Shanice. The girl's breath smelled like death.

In a flash, Mavis crouched on one foot, performed a swing kick with her left leg, and broke Shanice's leg at the knee. She crumpled to the ground, but she didn't cry out. Instead, she laughed long and hard. Reaching up to the car, she grabbed the handle and opened the door.

Mavis circled the car until she was standing about ten feet from the driver's door, with Matt and Kim quickly approaching and taking their places.

Shanice laughed as she pulled herself into the

running sedan, and she continued to laugh as she struggled with her dangling right leg, trying to get it out of the way.

All three maintained Kenpo positions of awareness and preparation, as they surrounded Shanice.

Shanice laughed at them. "So, you stop me for tonight, but I will be back!" she screamed. "You would be surprised at what I am capable of, and I'll come back with my guns swinging! You need to be prepared!"

Mavis and her friends stood, frozen to their spots, eyes glued to Shanice. She revved the engine, then suddenly she threw the sedan into gear and flipped the steering wheel in their direction.

Neither Matt nor Kim saw it coming, but Mavis did. "Run!" she shouted at them.

In only seconds they moved, saving their own lives by the skin on their backs. Mavis, though, was right in the line of fire. But just as the car was about to strike her, Mavis jumped into the air, and her feet landed solidly on the moving car. She scrambled like a spider up the hood, reached through the driver's side window, and began yanking as hard as she could at Shanice's hair. She was pulling it out in clumps and tossing them out the window.

"No!" Shanice screamed. "Not my hair!"

She quickly turned to the right, which flung Mavis off the car and to the ground, knocking the wind out of her. Instead of coming back to finish the job, Shanice continued into the night, screaming about her hair, and how could a girl do something like that to another girl.

At last, the taillights to the car faded, and after that, Shanice's shrill, horrid voice faded too.

Matt and Kim ran up to Mavis, who was already pushing herself into a sitting position.

"Are you okay, Babe?"

"Yeah, Mav," Kim said. "You hit hard, I'm telling you."

Mavis nodded and slowly began to rise to her feet, with Matt's help. "Yeah, I'll have a bruise that will never go away, but I'm pretty sure we got rid of Shanice for now." Mavis turned to Kim.

"How is she getting away with this crap?" Kim asked in a voice filled with disbelief.

"I guess it's true what they say: money can buy anything, and everyone has a price. I'll bet her mom and dad are rolling over in their graves."

Kim shrugged, a sheepish look on her face. "Sorry, Mavis. It was such a… hairy situation."

The three of them burst out in laughter, then made their way across the football field to the convertible, arm in arm. In the distance, they could hear sirens, but none of them cared.

Just like that, the senior prom was history.

CHAPTER 31

The sun was coming up over the Pointe in oranges, reds, yellows, purples, and blues. It was beautiful, and the sight of it only proved to make Toledo and the surrounding area look innocent, still, and serene. Mavis, Matt, and Kim sitting silently in the small white convertible at the top of the Pointe knew that the area was anything but peaceful. They didn't know if the chaos was still flying, or it had died down, but right now none of them were interested in finding out. They were happy and content right where they were.

They had been parked there, sitting quietly, no one speaking a word, since leaving the high school right around 10:45 the night before. They had all been thinking about the same thing as they watched the police lights swarm to the high school. They were wondering what the cops were thinking when the only dead bodies they found had been the walking dead. It was going to start something a bit crazy in Greenville, but Mavis was pretty sure that it would be explained away in some crazy way. By the end of summer, the entire incident would be nothing but an urban legend, especially after the three of them got done changing the story here and there in passing.

They all went back to looking at the sunrise.

Another five minutes passed when Kim suddenly spoke up. "Do you think they caught Shanice?"

Mavis didn't even have to hesitate with her answer. "Nope."

Matt turned to her from the driver's seat. "Why not? They could have nabbed her speeding out on their way in."

She shook her head. "Nah. They were too far out when she was out of site. She's out there... somewhere. Probably somewhere to find some new members for her sick family."

Kim's voice was barely more than a whisper. "What would stop her from staying around here?"

Matt chuckled. "She won't do that. Now they'll be looking for Shanice with every color hair possible."

The three of them laughed at his joke, but they knew he was right. Toledo, Greenville... heck, anywhere in Ohio or even the states was going to be a problem for Shanice.

There was a lull of several minutes in the conversation, then Matt turned to Mavis and took her by the hand. "You were so good, jumping on the hood like that. And ripping her hair out... I've never seen anything so funny in my entire life."

"Yeah," Kim agreed. "And you know how vain that little floozy has always been made it even funnier. You rocked, Mav."

"And you were sexy, too," Matt finished.

Kim made a sound like she was puking. "Come on, you guys, really? After all that you wanna go all goofy on me. I mean, it would be different if I had a guy, but wait 'til I'm out of the car, okay."

Mavis swung around with a smile on her face. "What about Tony?" she purred teasingly. "I hope this half-a-dance turns out to be more than a one-night stand."

Kim turned deep red. "Knock it off. If you must know, we have a date for next Friday. We're going to see that new zombie movie down at the multiplex."

Mavis' mouth fell open dramatically. "You're going with him to a zombie movie? Don't you think that's a little forward for a first date? I mean, after all…" She proceeded to gesture toward herself with her thumb.

Kim shook her head. "I don't think so. I told him, straight up, if you want to date me, you're going to have to muster a very deep affection for all things zombie."

Matt glanced at Mavis, then they both looked at Kim and shook their heads. "You're a sick girl, Kim. A sick, sick girl."

Changing the subject, Mavis took a deep breath and said, "Well, I think we'd better be getting back. Mom's going to be just getting up, and I want her to hear what happened from us, not from the news or the papers."

"Well, I was supposed to be staying with you, so I'm good to have your back," Kim replied. "What about you, Matt?"

"I'm with the both of you."

The sun rose further into the sky, so Matt started the

convertible and backed out of the gravel lot that made up the Pointe. They made their way down the steep gravel road that wrapped around the tiny mountain. Mavis had her window down, her head back, and her eyes closed. She was letting the sunshine on her face, and she was breathing in the crisp morning air. Considering the state of her body, and the garbage that her archenemy had put her through, Mavis felt spectacular!

They would have to give police reports. If the cops asked where they had been, they would say they took off once the dance ended.

As they drove, Mavis filled in her pals on the story, and together they rehearsed it, each telling it in their own words until they were comfortable. They laughed a few times at the comedy of it, but mostly, in the back of their minds, they were wondering where and when Shanice would turn up next.

But for now, it was just an amazing feeling to have true friends.

ENTREATY

This book was made possible by reviews from readers like you. Reviews fuel my creativity. If you enjoyed this novel, I implore you to please write a review and share your experience on the retailer's website. The livelihood for authors is entirely dependent on reviews, and I must say, it is the largest obstacle as a struggling author that I have encountered. Please tell a friend, tell a loved one about this read. With your help, I will be one step closer to overcoming this obstacle. In return, I thank you from the bottom of my heart, and sincerely appreciate your time and effort.

Humbled, with gratitude,

R.W.K. Clark

ABOUT THE AUTHOR

I am a father of two beautiful children, Jon and Kim. They are my motivating forces; they are the lighthouse in this vast ocean. In my life, they are the air that I breathe; they are the oasis in this desert of uncertainty. They are my greatest joy in life and my number one priority. I have a long list of hobbies, and I attribute that to my lust for life! I like to surround myself with positive people, who share the same interests. Family values, the arts, outdoors, nature, and travel are tops on my list. I embrace attending cultural and artistic events because I believe dramatic self-expression is the window to the soul. I wear my heart on my sleeve, and I still believe in chivalry, and I always treat people the way I want to be treated.

www.rwkclark.com

www.ingramcontent.com/pod-product-compliance
Lightning Source LLC
Chambersburg PA
CBHW020950180626
46814CB00003B/1014